J.V. KADE

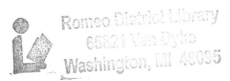

DIAL BOOKS
an imprint of Penguin Group (USA) LLC

DIAL BOOKS

Published by the Penguin Group

Penguin Group (USA) LLC

375 Hudson Street

New York, New York 10014

USA/Canada/UK/Ireland/Australia/New Zealand/India/South Africa/China

penguin.com

A Penguin Random House Company

Kade, J. V.

The meta-rise / J. V. Kade.

pages cm   Sequel to: Bot Wars.

Summary: A boy fights to stop an evil robot from taking over the futuristic
world where humans and robots are at war over robot civil rights.

ISBN 978-0-8037-3861-4 (hardcover)

[1. Robots—Fiction. 2. War—Fiction. 3. Science fiction.] I. Title.

PZ7.K116462Me 2014   [Fic]—dc23   2013033243

Printed in the United States of America

1 3 5 7 9 10 8 6 4 2

Designed by Mina Chung · Text set in Perrywood MT Std

To Eric—
This one is for the bearphers

UNITED DISTRICTS OF AMERICA

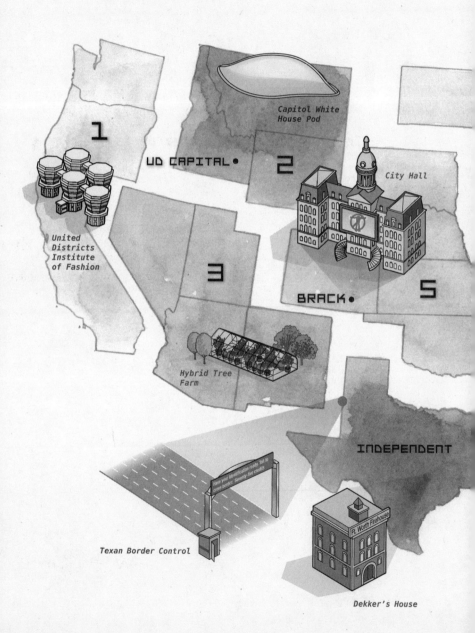

Capitol White House Pod

UD CAPITAL•

City Hall

1

2

United Districts Institute of Fashion

3

BRACK•

5

Hybrid Tree Farm

INDEPENDENT

Texan Border Control

Ft. Worth Firehouse

Dekker's House

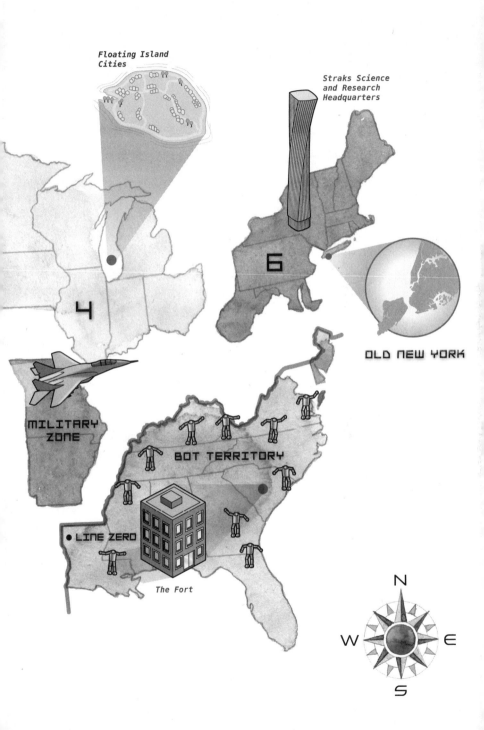

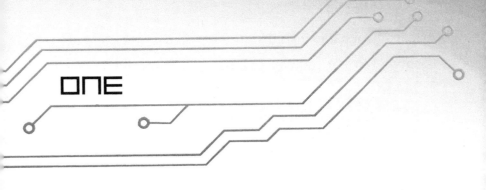

ONE

MY DAD IS half machine. My brother has a prosthetic leg. And one of my best friends here in Bot Territory is a robot.

I never thought I'd say this, but in just three months I've gone from thinking robots were the enemy to feeling like I need a robotic hand just to fit in.

When I tell my friend Vee this, she snorts and then starts gagging on the pizza pop she's eating, which causes Merril, the giant, barrel-chested bot cook, to swoop in and give Vee the Heimlich. Overhead, our building's new alarm system starts blaring through the speakers. "Human choking in dining room. Foreign object lodged in throat."

Merril moves to wrap his arms around Vee, but she dodges him and says, "I'm fine, jam it!" before trailing off in another round of coughs.

"Human choking," the alarm says again and I run to

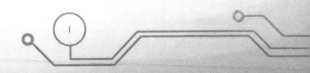

the control panel installed in the wall near the elevator. I punch in the code Scissor taught me and the system quiets.

When I come back into the dining room, Merril is still standing there staring at Vee like he's prepared for her to spontaneously choke on her own spit. He's worried, even though the chicken tenders he's frying in the kitchen are burning.

Vee is more important. For most of the bots I've met, it's the same thing. They care more about their human friends than they do anything else.

"I'm fine," Vee says again, and Merril finally saunters off, his footsteps *ting-ting*-ing against the concrete floor. Scissor, our mechanic robot, has been bugging him to let her upgrade his feet, since a lot of bots are turning to silicone foot pads so their steps aren't so loud. But Merril says he likes the sound.

"I hate that new alarm system," Vee says.

Scissor installed the system a few weeks ago, after my dad requested it. It keeps constant watch over the entire building, and all of its inhabitants, robot and human, just in case something should go wrong.

It's my dad's way of being overprotective, which is nice and all, but also annoying.

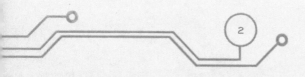

Vee and I sit back down with our remaining pizza pops. We're at the big dining room table in the middle of my dad's building. Everyone calls the building the Fort. It has all these cool nooks and crevices. And there are rope bridges. It's pretty much the best place ever. A lot better than the tiny house my older brother, Po, and I lived in, back before we moved to Bot Territory with Dad.

Even though I've only known Vee for a few months, I consider her my best *human* friend on this side of the border. Since moving to Bot Territory from the United Districts, my life has changed a space ton. LT, my bot friend, says my life is kinda like the metamorphosis of a caterpillar, because it starts out being ugly and lumpy and kinda hideous, and then it wraps itself in a cocoon and becomes a butterfly. He didn't say it in those words, but I know that's what he meant. And anyway, I don't think he knows what he's talking about. It's Po who got the wings, if we're continuing on with the whole metaphor business.

Which is even more obvious by the *RIDER* magazine sitting on the table in front of Vee. Po's face is on the cover, and the animated image transitions from a smiling Po, to a smiling-*bigger* Po, to a serious-faced

Po. The headline below him reads: "St. Kroix takes the world by storm, one freedom speech at a time."

When *RIDER* magazine called to ask him for an interview, Po couldn't stop talking about himself in the third person for weeks.

Like he's so important.

Vee sets her elbows on the table and leans toward me. "Let's go back to that thing you were saying. You know, that thing about how you wish you were part robot."

"I was kidding!" But secretly I wasn't. Fact is, lately it seems like everyone I pass in Line Zero, the town in Bot Territory where I live, has a robot part. It's like the thing to do here. You go to the upgrade shop, you pick out what you want from the display, and a week later you've got a robot arm or a leg or an optical implant that can sync to your Link. I heard you can even make phone calls on the implant.

It's pretty wrenched if you ask me.

But then you're stuck with the upgrade for the rest of your life. It's not like they can reattach the arm they took off. Which makes me wonder what they do with those arms.

"Think about it," Vee says after taking a gulp of juice.

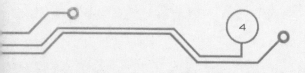

"What if you were picking your nose and put too much force behind it and accidentally poked yourself in the brain?"

"Like that's even possible."

"It could be."

"Theoretically, it is," Merril says, and Vee gives me a smug grin, so I stick out my tongue at her.

"What's the plan for today?" she asks a second later.

I chomp on my pizza pop. "I don't know. We could harass Po and Marsi."

Vee rolls her eyes. "I am so sick of those two slobbering all over each other."

I grimace. "Using the words *Po* and *slobbering* in the same sentence gears me out."

"It gears me out too." Vee looks over her shoulder at Merril in the kitchen, then lowers her voice when she turns back to me. "Listen. I heard Po telling Marsi that he has a Meta-Rise meeting this afternoon in the old library downtown."

At the mention of the Meta-Rise, I sit up straighter. "And you waited until now to tell me?"

Vee tilts her head, which makes her hair glow orange in the sunlight pouring through the window. She dyes her hair with special dye so that the color changes

depending on the light that surrounds her. A few minutes ago, it almost looked green.

"The meeting isn't until one o'clock," she says. "I had plenty of time to tell you."

My dad calls the Meta-Rise the bot/human alliance. It's this group of people and bots who believe in living together peacefully, unlike the UD, which still believes robots are the enemy, that they've become too much like humans. Robots aren't allowed in the UD. They're terminated upon capture.

My dad, Robert St. Kroix, is the leader of the Meta-Rise. He's the best man for the job, not only because he's top gear, but also because he's half man, half robot, and if anyone can understand both sides of the conflict, it's him.

Vee and I want to be members of the Meta-Rise, but our dads think we're too young.

It's lame.

"So," I whisper back to Vee, "are we going?"

"What do you think?"

"Yes."

She nods, and her ponytail swings forward. "That's the right answer, FishKid."

I frown. "Why can't you call me Trout like everyone else?"

"Because where's the fun in being like everyone else?"

"I'll tell you what's not fun. Being called FishKid."

"Oh, but it's such a cracked name. Hey, what do you think they'd call you if you got a robot part? FishBot?" She bursts out laughing. "That's even better. I fully support you upgrading."

I grumble as we leave the kitchen.

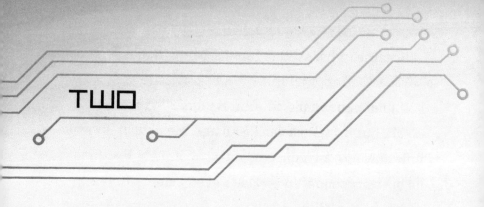

TWO

THING ABOUT VEE is, she can get just about anywhere, but it doesn't usually involve a door.

Thankfully, I'm good at climbing.

I find a foothold in the old pitted brick of the back of the library and push myself up. There's a ladder—a rusted fire escape—but the bottom half rusted off probably a bazillion years ago, so I have to scale the wall halfway up to pull the rest of the fire escape down.

"Hurry," Vee says. "It's almost one o'clock."

Sweat beads on my forehead as the sun blasts down. I'm drenched, and we've only been outside for less than twenty minutes. The temperatures have been in the high nineties the last week. I call it sweaty-armpit weather. Scissor calls it whir weather, because of the constant whirring noise the bots' cooling systems make.

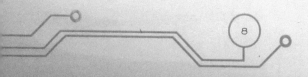

"I *am* hurrying," I call down.

I navigate another three feet and reach for the ladder. I'm able to grab hold of the last ladder rung and throw myself onto it. Rust flakes off the metal, raining into my hair. My added weight dislodges the ladder and then I'm falling.

When the ladder reaches the end of its rail, it snaps back, and jerks me loose. I sail to the ground, hitting the pavement with a thud.

I only dropped about four feet, but that was four feet too many.

"Ouch," I moan.

Vee peers over on top of me. "There you go, falling again."

I roll onto all fours. "You're welcome for the ladder."

"Thanks for the ladder," she mock-echoes.

Vee positions an empty crate beneath the ladder, to give her another foot of height, and latches on to the bottom rung. From there she pulls herself up without much trouble.

We make it to the roof in hardly any time at all. The air up here is even hotter, if that's possible, so that it feels like I'm swimming in it. The humidity sticks to my skin. I'm from 5th District, what used to be Colorado. Line

Zero is in what used to be Louisiana. I'm not used to the southern weather yet. Maybe I never will be.

"Now where?" I ask, wiping the sweat from beneath my nose with the back of my hand.

"Over here." Vee leads me to a door on the far side of the roof and slowly, quietly, pops open the latch.

We enter into a stairwell and press our backs against the wall and listen. It's silent for a long time, so we head down.

"Which floor are they on?" I whisper.

"Second floor, I think."

When we reach it, we pull the door open and peek into another hallway. I see Po come off the elevator and head left.

I shrink back, but hold the door open a crack so it doesn't click closed, alerting Po.

"That was close," Vee says.

I nod, wait a beat. "So, I take it we go left?"

Vee snorts. "You would make a terrible spy."

"What?"

"If we go left, we'll walk right into their meeting, and if we do that, our dads will kick us out."

"Then how are we going to listen to the meeting?"

The smile that spreads across Vee's face makes her

look like a maniacal clown. "Follow me, gearbox, and I'll show you."

When the hallway is clear, we sprint to the right, keeping close to the wall, in case we need to duck inside another room for cover. We make it around the next corner and Vee points us to the right again.

"Third door on the left," she says.

The door is unlocked. We go inside and find a surveillance room.

"Are you kidding me?" I say.

"What?" Vee looks confused.

"This is the worst place to hide out when listening in on super-secret meetings."

Vee takes a seat in the old swivel chair in the center of the room. The gears inside shriek as she turns around. "You're forgetting I'm Parker Dade's daughter."

Parker is Dad's closest friend and is in charge of planning escape and rescue routes from the UD to Bot Territory.

"So?" I answer.

"So, I know how my dad operates. He would have checked here first thing, to make sure the system was down. The library has been empty for a while, so it's

not like there was going to be anyone coming in and out. Dad would have checked the security system, and once he was sure it was off, he would have given your dad the okay.

"Which means we're free to hang out as long as we like and"—she presses a series of buttons on the control panel and the monitors embedded in the wall come to life—"listen in on the super-secret meeting."

The audio system boots up and I immediately recognize Dad's voice.

"Thanks for meeting us here," he says, and I find him on the farthest monitor on the left. He's in a room surrounded by empty bookcases, standing at the head of a rectangular table. Each seat at the table is occupied by someone from the Meta-Rise. There's Parker and LT, and the rest of Dad's security team, as well as Jules, Cole, and a few others I don't know.

Po is sitting between Jules and Parker, picking at a gouge in the table, looking bored. I would give anything in the world to be in his spot right now. I want to be a member of the Meta-Rise so badly, I dream about it in my sleep. And here Po is, automatically granted access to the secret meetings, and he doesn't even care. Sometimes I hate how easy everything is for Po.

I mean, yeah, okay, so he lost his leg in the war, but somehow, in the two months that we've been in Bot Territory, even the bum leg has made Po more wrenched. There's even a "Po St. Kroix" upgrade at the upgrade shop. People pay a lot of creds to have a bum leg just like my brother.

Which is just dumb if you ask me. Out of all the upgrades you can get, why would you pay creds for a bum leg?

"I apologize for the secret location," Dad says. When he turns his head, the half of his face that was replaced with a metal plate gleams in the overhead light. "I wanted to be sure we weren't interrupted."

I wonder if he suspects Vee and I are desperate to know what's going on At All Times. And if he moved the Meta-Rise meeting to the library hoping to avoid us. He caught us eavesdropping a week ago, when the Meta-Rise met to discuss the UD's recent movements, and President Callo's latest speech.

Jules, Dad's tech advisor, said Callo is trying to do damage control after the UD attacked Edge Flats, Texas, two months ago. Callo blamed it on Sandra "Beard" Hopper, who was the head of Congress at the time, but Vee and I secretly wonder if he knew about the attack all along. The UD doesn't want to live peacefully with robots, and I think they're willing to do anything to keep bots as nothing more than machine slaves.

Beard was going to pin the blame for the attack on Dad, and the Meta-Rise, hoping to turn the rest of the UD against robots for good.

Thankfully, we stopped the attack before it got really bad, and ever since then Callo has been trying to make it sound like he's neutral on the whole thing.

"As you all know," Dad goes on, folding his arms across his chest, "we've been hearing from some of our outlying sources that Old New York has been busier than normal. And"—he glances at Parker—"from what we've dug up, it seems to be true. We recently received a report that ten thousand ThinkChips were purchased on the black market and shipped into Old New York last week."

Voices rise around the room, but Dad talks over them. "I don't want anyone alarmed yet. That's why we haven't spoken about it publicly, but . . ." Dad trails off and LT stands.

He's a few inches taller than Dad, with sharp shoulders, wide eyes, and a dented, scraped chest plate the color of mushed peas. The rest of him is plain robot-

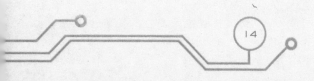

grade melorra steel. He doesn't have a lot of the flashy upgrades most other robots do. I like that about him.

LT clears his throat. "One of our allies in ONY has confirmed Ratch is present in the city, though we have been unable to identify if he is connected to the Think-Chips."

Hearing Ratch's name makes all the hairs on the back of my neck stand up.

Ratch was LT's best friend, and part of Dad's team. Until he turned on us in the middle of City Hall in the UD when we were trying to rescue Po. I still have nightmares about him, about his glowing band of orange eyes staring at me, like he's using his robot powers to see through my skin, to my bones, to see my human weaknesses.

"We *have* been able to confirm, however," LT goes on, "that Ratch is plotting some kind of attack on the Meta-Rise."

Murmurs spread through the room.

Vee and I glance at each other, wide-eyed.

"We do not know what kind of attack it will be," LT goes on, "or when it will take place. What we do know is that it will most likely be aimed at the Meta-Rise leader."

All eyes turn to Dad.

The blood drains from my face. My heart ka-thumps in my ears. I look at Po, to see his reaction. He doesn't look surprised at all. It's like he already knew this secret.

"Why you?" Cole asks Dad. "Why attack the Meta-Rise at all? We're on the side of the robots."

Dad pulls in a breath and shoves his hands in his pants pockets. "Most likely he wants to show the robot race that I'm weak."

"Which you aren't," Po says, but directs it at the room.

"We have a defense already in place," Dad says. "We have some of the best security, and the best tech team. Ratch isn't getting anywhere near us. You can count on that.

"I just wanted to be sure you were all aware of what's going on. I wanted you to hear it from me first. And if you gain any new information, or see anything suspicious, please contact me immediately. For the time being, please do not disclose anything you've heard here, or what you may hear out there."

After Dad answers a few more questions from other members, he calls the meeting to an end. Everyone except Dad, Parker, LT, Jules, and Po leaves the room.

Jules is the first to speak after the door is shut behind a departing Meta-Rise member. "So what do you really think about all this?"

"What do I really think?" Dad echoes as he paces to the window and peers out. From the angle of the camera, I can only see him from the neck down, but I can hear the worry in his voice when he speaks.

"I think we need to watch our backs," Dad answers. "Whatever Ratch is up to, it won't be good."

THREE

"**THIS IS BAD**. This is bad. This is bad."

I keep repeating the same phrase over and over again as Vee and I shuffle toward home.

"Hey," she says, hooking her arm through mine to spin me toward her. "This is your dad we're talking about. Robert St. Kroix. Leader of the Meta-Rise. Ratch is cracked if he thinks he can threaten your dad and get away with it."

My breath is coming too quickly, like I'm a bull about to charge. Except, instead of being steaming mad, I'm a blubbery mess of panic.

"What if something happens to my dad?" I say, echoing the same fears I had two months ago when the UD was trying to get my dad to turn himself in.

Vee puts her hands on either side of my face and forces me to look at her. Her hair is dark blue now, and her eyes are big and bright in the sunlight. "Nothing is going to happen to him."

I nod, but I don't know if I believe it. What if there's something Dad knows that he's not telling the team? What if he told Po? What if they're trying to keep it from me?

Later, after Vee has gone home, I go into town to find Po. Even though my brother is good at keeping secrets—after all, he kept the secret about Dad being alive and living in Bot Territory from me for a long time—I think I might be able to guilt him into sharing *something* about Ratch and the ThinkChips, if there is any more to know.

The streets are bustling with activity, since it's a weekend, and the sun has gone down enough to allow the temperature to cool off. I pass a group of people and bots walking down the sidewalk. The people are eating ice-cream cones, and the bots are guzzling Life Water— the preferred drink of robots. I don't know what's in it, but my dad drinks it, so it must not taste too bad. Dad still has human taste buds, even though his stomach has been replaced with a robotic system.

Dad was injured during the wars. LT and Ratch rescued him, and Scissor put him back together. A lot of his human body had to be replaced with robot parts, in order to save him.

At first, when I saw him, I geared out. But then I realized Dad was still Dad, and I was just happy he was safe.

I pause for a streetlight at the next intersection. Several hover cars whiz past on the rails. A few kids on hoverboards fly by in the hoverboard lane, their eyes hidden behind riding sunglasses. The glasses are a single band that stretch across their eyes. The lenses are mirrored, and when the kid closest to the curb zooms past me, the glasses catch the reflection of the orange brick building behind me. For a second, the glasses are nothing but a band of orange and I'm immediately reminded of Ratch and his band of eyes.

My stomach drops to my feet.

Ratch is here, my brain says. *He's here to hurt Dad.*

I take a step back, run into a robot, whose spindly machine hands wrap around my arm to steady me. I suck in a breath, jerk away, slam into a woman, bounce back, then topple over a bench.

Before I know it, I'm staring at the darkening sky overhead, blinking back tears of pain. I whacked my side on the bench's seat, then smashed my hip when I finally hit the sidewalk.

"Are you all right?" a robot asks.

The woman I ran into peers down at me. "Are you okay? I didn't see you coming!"

"I'm fine," I say, but my voice shakes. I manage to roll onto my knees and just as I'm pushing myself to my feet, a hand latches on to me and helps me up.

It's Po.

"You okay, little bro?" he asks.

Whispers spread through the growing crowd. Back in Brack, whenever someone whispered around me, I knew it had to do with one of two things: Either it was about my missing dad and my dead mom, or it was about how I was a total drain clogger.

But now I know it has nothing to do with the first thing. Because here my dad is a hero, and my brother is too. It could be that everyone watching thinks I'm lame, but somehow I don't think that's it either.

Because they're all staring at Po.

In the months we've been in Bot Territory, he's changed a lot, but for the better. Back in Brack, he worked long hours, and never ate right, so he was skinny, like me. He never did much with his hair because we couldn't afford to go to a place to get it cut, so Po just let it grow out, and then buzzed it off with a clipper at the beginning of every spring.

Our clothes were secondhand, bought from whatever thrift store we stumbled into.

But now . . . now my brother is wrenched.

Not only does everyone in Bot Territory look at him like a megastar, because of his freedom speech after the attack on Edge Flats, but they also admire him because he's the son of the leader of the Meta-Rise, which makes him kinda like a prince. Next in line for the throne and all of that stuff.

He's gotten a ton of new clothes lately. Stores just send him stuff for free, because they know if Po is spotted wearing their brands, everyone else will buy those clothes too, to look like him.

Today he's wearing River jeans. They're adjustable, so he can wear them either fitted or baggy with the press of a button. Now they're just slightly baggy, and tucked into untied black combat boots. His T-shirt has embedded neon threads in the collar, and with the sun setting, the threads are just starting to glow neon green, illuminating his face.

His hair has been cut recently, but it's sticking out every which way, like he just rolled out of bed and didn't bother fixing it. I know that's not true, because he took up the bathroom for an hour messing with his

hair and whatever greasy paste he was putting in it. It smelled like roses and fresh-cut grass. Basically like an old lady mowing the lawn.

So, even though I just fell flat on my butt in the middle of town, it isn't me people are paying attention to, it's my brother.

"I'm okay," I repeat, even though my butt feels like it's on fire.

"You sure?" Po asks. He nods at the park across the street. "I was sitting over there when I saw you stop for the streetlight. You looked like you were gearing out." He narrows his eyes, like he's examining me. "What happened?"

"Nothing. I'm just clumsy. You know that." Which is true. Even though I hate admitting to it, it's the best excuse I got. I'm not going to tell Po that for a second I thought I saw Ratch, that I was afraid he was here to hurt Dad.

Po shoves his hands in his pants pockets, which makes his new arm muscles look bigger. Out of the corner of my eye, I see a bunch of girls whispering and giggling and pointing at Po.

My brother's new fame makes me want to gag.

Especially when girls do this kind of thing, and act

like he's a rock star, like the pop singer Tanner Waylon.

I suddenly don't feel like talking to Po, or to anyone, no matter how much I want to know about Ratch and his threat.

"I *said* I was fine," I say again, and turn around and bolt for home.

FOUR

ON MONDAY, I drag myself out of bed just in time to eat a quick breakfast before school. I didn't come out of my room much the rest of the weekend, mostly because I was embarrassed about what happened in the town center, and maybe a little bit annoyed at Po for being . . . well, Po.

And, even more annoying than Po being Po was the fact that Dad went about his business for the rest of the weekend like nothing at all had changed. Like one of the most cracked robots hadn't threatened his life.

I plop down across from Marsi at the table, trying to ignore my brother's jokes about me being a vampire, and the sunlight burning my flesh. Marsi hands me a packet of brown sugar and I tear it open, dumping the whole thing on top of my oatmeal. Next, she slides the pitcher of milk my way and I add a splash before stirring it all together.

Po groans. "You're babying him, you know."

"I am not," Marsi argues.

"Yeah, she is not," I say, but secretly I know she is. I don't like it when Po or my dad treats me like a kid, but when Marsi does it . . . well, it's like the mother I never had. My mom died when I was only two years old. I don't even remember her. Sometimes I have to stare at a picture of her for a few minutes just to remember what she looked like.

Po shakes his head and turns away from us, grabbing the nearest SimPad. He prompts it, and taps in a quick command, bringing up the local feed. It plays a mixture of news reports and pop culture shows.

When the holo projector starts up, it displays a 3-D image of the baseball game that went on last night in Ripley Park. It's a robot and human league, with most teams made up of equal parts of both. The feed replays the winning hit made by a girl a few years older than Po. The bat slams into the ball and the ball goes sailing across the field, disappearing out of sight. The crowd cheers.

Po sips from his cup of coffee as the feed switches to a new story. I look away, shoveling in the rest of my oatmeal, when Po spits lukewarm coffee all over the place and bursts out laughing.

"Hey!" I shout. "Why did you do that?"

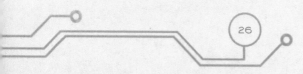

He can't stop laughing enough to talk. Marsi sighs and gestures to the SimPad.

I look over. There I am, in tiny 3-D holo form, slamming into a bench and falling to the sidewalk on my butt. The feed replays the footage again in slow-mo, which makes my face look like it's made out of cheese curds.

Someone recorded me falling Saturday night in the town center. And now they're playing it on the news.

I groan. "Great."

The footage zooms out and narrows in on Po running across the street to rescue me. The girl who hosts the show says, "Ladies, just watch. Watch and weep."

The footage slows down again. Po's hair blows in the wind. His face is illuminated with the neon implants in his shirt. His arms are pumping by his sides. Whoever edited the footage added a dozen red hearts above Po's head and they trail after him like a cloud of butterflies.

"Where has this boy been my whole life?" the host says. "Po St. Kroix, if you're listening, call me!" The footage cuts out and the live cameras flick to the host. In 3-D holo form, it's like she's smiling right at Po from the center of our dining room table.

"Ugh," I say, and prompt the SimPad to hibernate. "I don't know why they think you're so special."

Po grins. "When you got it, you got it."

Marsi chuckles and points at the front of his shirt. "If only they could see you now."

Po looks down. There is a dribbled coffee stain down the front of him. Now I'm the one laughing. Marsi winks at me.

"You two really like ganging up on me, don't you?" Po says.

"Uh, yeah," I say.

"Yes," Marsi says.

Po shoves away from the table and disappears down the hallway, probably to change his shirt. Marsi goes to the kitchen and comes back a second later with a wet rag to help me clean up. Thankfully, Po's blast of coffee didn't hit my clothes.

"Thanks," I say.

She ruffles my hair as she leaves. "You're welcome, Aidan."

I grin. Hardly anyone calls me by my real name. It sounds cool when Marsi does it. Like I'm more than just Po's little brother. More than just a kid.

I make it into class thirty-three seconds before the bell rings and drop into my seat next to Vee. Today, her hair

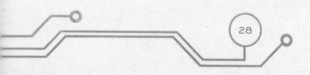

is tied back in a high ponytail. The sides of her head have recently been shaved, giving her a really long Mohawk. In the sunny classroom, her hair is bright pink with strands of copper. When she waves at me, the square wire bracelets on her wrists clack together.

"Cutting it close," she says.

"Always."

Our teacher, Kenpo, walks in and calls hello. He's a robot with a head shaped like a fish, with big, protruding eyes. His lips too are big, his nose small in comparison. Vee calls him my robot soul brother, because I'm nicknamed after a fish, and because our teacher looks like one.

Soul brother or not, I like Kenpo. Vee says he's new to the school this year, but he seems like he's been teaching forever, like he knows how to make lessons fun. He has a laid-back teaching style, unlike my instructors back in 5th District, who liked to talk for the entire hour of class and then assign a space ton of homework.

When Dad first told me I had to sign up for school in Line Zero, I was mega annoyed. I guess a part of me had thought (or hoped) that school didn't exist in Bot Territory, and if it did, it was optional. I guess some things never change.

But school in Line Zero is way different than school in the UD. For one, it's not every day. We only go three days a week. The rest of the week, we're supposed to "enjoy the freedom to experience life firsthand." It says so in the school handbook.

Also, classes aren't scheduled around the five basic subjects, with tests and pop quizzes and exams. Kenpo lets us pick the topics we want to learn about.

This week, we're studying the Robot Wars. I picked that one. But since it's a subject that's been covered a lot in the past, Kenpo decided to focus solely on the rise of the Robot Wars, particularly the first few months before the war, and the first few months just after it started.

As always, he gives the class a few minutes to hang out after the bell while he gets the day's lesson organized. I think today we're watching a documentary.

The kid in front of me, Yan, turns around in his seat and rests his arms on my desk. "What's cracking, Trout?"

I shrug. "Nothing. You?"

Yan shrugs too. "Not much. Hey, are you going to the September Festival?"

I glance over at Vee. "What's that?"

"Oh," she says. "I forgot to tell you. It's an annual thing. Every September. Obviously. It's kinda like a carnival. There will be rides and games and stuff."

"And food," Yan adds. "Lots and lots of food."

"When is it?"

"Next weekend," Vee answers.

"I'll be there."

Yan grins, and as he does, Vee and I notice something new about him. "You got neon tooth implants!" I say.

"I am so jealous," Vee says, wide-eyed. "When did you get those?"

"This weekend. Kila, ya?"

"Totally!" Vee says.

It takes me a second to decipher what Yan meant. *Kila* is a word the kids use around here, which is apparently a shortened Filipino word for *great*. I think that's what it is, anyway. Yan's grandparents came from the Philippines and were successful business owners in Line Zero before the wars. They still are, though business is different now that Bot Territory is separate from the UD.

Everyone does what Yan does around here, so *kila* is a word I'm hearing a lot more now that I'm in school.

I kinda like it. I especially like Yan. Even though he's

one of the most popular kids here, he doesn't act like it. He talks to everyone. And was really nice to me when I first started at the junior high.

"Let me see them again," I say, and Yan opens his mouth wider. The neon implants are tiny chips glued to his molars, kinda like braces. He got blue and green.

"Whoa," I say. "That is wrenched."

"Did it hurt?" Vee asks.

"Nah." Yan makes a gun with his fingers and points it at his jaw. "Just a quick bip-bip and it was done. You two should get an upgrade, ya?"

"Trout wants a robot part." Vee nudges me with her boot.

I frown her way, because I told her that in secret, and I'm not sure I want anyone knowing I want robot parts.

"What would you get?" Yan asks.

I shrug, all nonchalant. "Maybe just a hand or something."

"I get ya. The St. Kroix special!"

"No! Not that. I don't want to be like my dad," I argue, but deep down inside, I know I do want to be more like him. And like Po. Not only am I the odd man out in school, I'm also the odd man out in my own

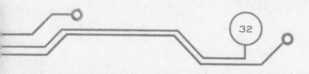

family. The only one of us that is still a hundred percent human. And being human isn't cool anymore.

Our teacher claps his hands. "Ladies and gentlemen, are we ready to get started?"

The class nods in agreement.

"Now, I want to forewarn you," Kenpo says. "This vid is not for the faint of heart. Particularly if you are extremely close with robots. I know many of you call a bot or two family. If you don't feel comfortable watching this documentary, you're more than welcome to go to the library." He pauses, and scans the class, but no one moves.

Yan whispers to me, "This is going to be the best vid they've ever shown in class."

Vee snorts and rolls her eyes. "Boys and their violence."

"All right. Here we go." Kenpo cues up the projector. Since the whole room is programmed to work together, the overhead lights turn off once the projector turns on. At first, there's nothing but a faint white light, then the entire room is transformed into a factory, so that it's like we're part of the history as it plays.

Everyone quiets as the audio kicks in. Kenpo goes to the far corner of the classroom, to his desk, and buries himself in grading papers.

The vid starts out with an intro about labor laws and the Machinery Tax Law, how both contributed to the start of the war.

A bot comes on screen. He's sitting in front of the camera, with nothing but a black wall behind him. "I don't know if anyone can pinpoint the exact moment things changed," he says. "No one can say the war began on a Thursday or a Monday. But if you look close enough, you can see the beginning stages. The layers to the conflict that built up over time.

"The undercover footage from Harvo Industries is a good example of where the foundation began."

The robot and the black background disappear, and the interior of a factory replaces him.

"Before the war gained ground," a voiceover says, "robot protests were happening all over the country. The very first one took place at Harvo Industries. The following events were what led to it."

The footage zeros in on a group of working bots.

A tall robot says, "I don't get why we're the ones busting our bones, but it's the boss who gets our wages."

"We're slave labor," another bot says. His holo image walks past me up the aisle of desks to the front of the room. He takes out a heavy stack of pre-cut metal sheets

from a cart and starts feeding them into the machine positioned near the classroom windows. "We put out the product. The master gets the profit. It's not right."

"If we start stirring up trouble, however," a smaller bot says, "the people of the United States will worry we've become too advanced. They'll worry their science fiction stories are no longer stories."

The bot next to her rests his hand on her shoulder. "Yes, but they need to realize we are no longer just machines, Mel. Take your request for an upgrade, for instance. Your joints are wearing down. You need a transplant and a few days off. Request denied. What does that say about us? About them? It says they believe we are disposable."

The feed blinks out. Large block letters flash across the front of the room.

THREE WEEKS LATER.

I can tell right away that the bots in this second clip are the same bots from the first. Mel works on one of the molding machines, feeding sheets of metal into the machine. When she steps back, a large stamp drops down with a thump, bending the metal into a perfect curve. Steam rises from the seams with a hiss. The stamp retracts. Mel pulls the molded sheet out and replaces it with a new one. She does this over and over again. It looks like tedious work, but I think everyone in the classroom knows something is going to happen soon enough.

Mel inserts a new sheet into the machine, but this time, she doesn't step back. Panic races across her face. "Oh no," she says. Her left arm isn't moving. The fingers are still clamped on the sheet of metal. She looks down at her feet. Her left leg is frozen in place.

"Help!" she shouts. "Someone, help!"

Something crunches in her leg and her knee bends forward at an odd angle.

My heart drums in my chest. I'm darting between the machine's stamp and Mel, hoping that she gets out of the way before the stamp comes down.

Footsteps thump behind me. The entire class turns around as a robot appears in the feed, bursting out of the back of the classroom wall. He's running to save Mel, but instead of feeling relief, I feel immediate, heart-crunching dread.

I know that robot.

That glowing band of orange eyes.

Ratch.

I leap out of my seat as the machine slams down. The classroom gasps.

It only takes one second for Mel to be destroyed.

Steam rises in the air as wires crack and pop and Ratch shouts at anyone close enough to hear him.

"Shut it down! Shut it down!"

Someone flips a lever and the stamp opens. Ratch is there to catch Mel as what's left of her body crumples to the floor. She's nothing but legs now, and a ball of crunched metal and torn wires above the waist.

She's gone. Just like that.

Ratch lets out a roar. Robots and humans run toward him. They try to take Mel out of his hands, but he won't let her go. He bows his head for several minutes until a factory foreman—a human—pulls a small stick-like object out of his pocket. Robots back away. The foreman presses his finger to the stick's button. The end lights up crimson. He shoves it into Ratch's neck and Ratch seizes up, his fingers curling into claws as an electrical current rushes through his limbs.

Ratch's whole body convulses, and then suddenly the vid cuts out and the classroom lights flick back on.

"Sorry!" Kenpo says. "I forgot . . ." He looks directly at me. "I'm sorry. It's been a while since I played that documentary."

"Trout, you okay?" Vee asks. I'm still pressed into the corner, unblinking. She, out of everyone, knows exactly why I geared out. Ratch turned on us. He left us for dead in the hands of the UD when we needed him the most.

I hated him.

I *do* hate him. He threatened to hurt my dad.

But right now I'm feeling all mixed up inside, like I'm not sure what's right and what's wrong.

Mostly I feel bad for Ratch because he watched Mel die in a factory accident that could have been avoided if only her joints had been replaced. She was his friend. And she died in his arms.

"Trout?" Kenpo says.

Everyone is staring at me.

"I'm fine," I mutter, and ease into my chair.

But I'm not. I'm more confused than I was before watching the vid. I thought I understood the Robot Wars. I thought I knew who the enemy was.

Now I feel like I don't know anything at all.

FIVE

"YOU SURE YOU'RE okay?" Vee asks.

We're lying on my bed staring up at the tricker ball hovering above us. It's this little brown ball that hangs in midair anywhere from one to ten seconds before dropping. Sometimes I'm not ready for it, and then it whacks me in the face when it comes down.

The last time we played, I had a bruised eye for a week. I only like playing because I like trying to beat Vee. She always wins at everything.

The ball hovers at least six feet above us now, whirring with its flying mechanism. My hands are tense at my sides, my feet curl in my shoes as I wait.

"I'm fine, Vee. Everyone needs to stop asking me."

Vee sighs. "You're a terrible liar."

The tricker ball drops. I snatch it out of the air. "Fine. You want to know the truth? I feel like Ratch is haunting me. It's like he's everywhere, trying to hurt everything I love. I feel like I'm about to go nuclear. Pretty soon my dad is going to have to lock me up in a mental institution."

I take in a breath. "I'm scared, though. Ratch is a robot, and he's strong and smart. Sometimes I worry that he's too strong, and too smart for our dads. They're tough, but do you think a human can really beat a robot?"

Vee rolls her head my way. "I do. I think our dads have something Ratch doesn't: They have friends, and loyal soldiers. And more than that, they're the good guys, and good guys always win."

"No they don't, Vee."

"This time they will."

I deactivate the tricker ball and set it aside. "You think our dads are gonna go after Ratch? To Old New York? You think they'll try to fight him before he attacks first?"

Vee shrugs. "Seems like a totally cracked idea, if you ask me. It'd be dumb to go up there without knowing what they're up against."

Old New York is supposed to be a friendly enough city. At least that's what Scissor told me, but I've heard a lot of talk on the UD news feed lately about ONY, about how worried the UD is. That ONY is populated

with rogue robots who want to take over. They think ONY is making more robots, *better* bots, to make an army for the next Bot Wars.

I heard my dad telling Po that he's worried that whatever is going on in ONY will reflect badly on us in Line Zero, since the UD citizens lump all of Bot Territory together, even though it spreads from what used to be New York, all the way south to the border of Texas.

Just like the old United States was different from state to state, so is Bot Territory. If there are rogue robots in ONY, they're nothing like us here in Line Zero.

I consider the robots here my friends, and some of them, even my family.

"Hey, I'll be right back. I'm going to the bathroom," I say.

Inside, I shut and lock the door behind me. The screen embedded in the vanity mirror is running footage of the latest baseball game. 2nd District won. Not surprising there.

After I'm done, I wash my hands in the sink, scanning the news feed as I do. "Breaking News," the feed says, in large red text. "Sources confirm, Congresswoman Heather Evans is missing from her Fourth District home. Ms. Evans was last seen yesterday afternoon when she returned to her condo after work. Her neighbor says she thought she heard Ms. Evans take her dog out for a walk sometime after dark, but is unsure as to whether Ms. Evans ever returned.

"Authorities are performing a search on all four Lake Michigan island cities, where Ms. Evans resides. The search will continue on the mainland later today. If you have any information regarding Heather Evans, or her whereabouts, please contact the UD Hotline at . . ."

The rest of the report is cut off by the house's intercom system announcing dinner.

I hurry out of the bathroom, my stomach grumbling at the thought of food.

Dad doesn't show for dinner. After Vee and I stuff our faces with Merril's grilled fish dinner, Vee says goodbye. One of her favorite shows is on tonight, and it's a show I have no interest in wasting sixty minutes of my life watching.

I go straight up to command center and find Dad in the center of the room, arms crossed over his chest. His team is spread around him. Some of them are working at their stations, their fingers zipping over their keyboards.

Jules is sitting in her desk chair, but it's turned around backward, her arms draped over the back of the chair.

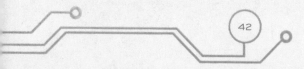

"There has to be footage somewhere," she says.

Dad nods and gestures to Cole. "Start scouring every feed within thirty miles of Heather's house, and check the Michigan shoreline feeds as well. Whoever grabbed her either escaped straight up—which would be caught on a camera somewhere—or they went to shore. If there's evidence, I want it."

Heather? I wonder if he's talking about Heather Evans, and then realize he must be because he mentioned Michigan, where Heather disappeared from.

"I'm on it, boss," Cole says with a nod, the laser implants in the bridge of his nose casting odd shadows across his face.

"As soon as you have something, even if it's a flicker on a darkened cam feed, I want to see it," Dad says.

As the tech team settles into their work, chatting amongst themselves, Parker pulls Dad and LT into the office beneath the loft area. No one has noticed me yet, so I nonchalantly but kinda stealthily make my way around the perimeter of the room and come up to the storage area behind the office. There are boxes stacked along the wall, giving me cover as I crouch near the vent that connects the main room with the office. Vee was the one who told me about the vent, and it's how we've listened in to many secret meetings.

Parker is the first one to speak. "Heather Evans is one of the four with a code, isn't she?"

Dad exhales and runs his robotic hand over his head, messing up his hair. Po does the same thing when he's frustrated. "Yeah," he finally says.

Parker curses beneath his breath.

"The good thing," LT adds, "is that she is the only one of the four missing. We have time to craft a plan."

"I don't know," Parker says. "If Ratch is stockpiling ThinkChips, he could be steps ahead of us already."

"*If* Ratch is the one who bought the chips," Dad points out. "ONY has been manufacturing bots for a while. This isn't news to us."

Parker snorts. "Yeah, but not ten thousand at once. ONY isn't that ambitious."

"He is right," LT says. "ONY puts out a thousand new robots a year, at most."

The office goes quiet for a beat, then Parker says, "Who else does he need to open the facility?"

I frown. What facility?

The desk chair groans as Dad sits. "President Callo. Nathaniel Rix. And Georgette Winters, provided she's still alive. She's been off the grid for years. I don't know who her backup is. It'd take some time to find out who would be activated in the event of her death."

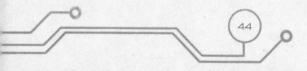

Backup. Activated. I suddenly wish Vee were here to help me make sense of everything.

I burn the names into my brain, knowing they'll be important later.

But what does Tellie Rix's dad have to do with any of this?

"Can we get someone to watch the three remaining?" Dad asks. "We still have someone inside the UD? Or inside Brack?"

"We do," Parker answers. "The president is going to be a tough one to get to. And it'll be even harder putting a detail on him without being noticed. I'll look into Georgette and see what I can dig up."

"Have someone check in on Rix too," Dad adds.

"I'll get on it now."

The door to the office opens and closes. I squish myself real small so Parker doesn't see me when he leaves.

After a minute, I sit up again and press my ear to the metal grate on the vent. LT is speaking. "This does not sit well with me, Robert."

"It doesn't sit well with me either." Dad's footsteps head for the office door as he continues talking to LT.

I scramble from my hiding spot, and as I do, I accidentally knock over a tower of boxes. Files spill out onto the floor. Dad stops. His robot heart glows yellow in the dim lighting beneath the loft area. Suddenly everyone is looking at me.

"What are you doing?" Dad asks.

"Ummm, nothing?" I raise my eyebrows, and realize too late that it sounds (and looks) like I'm asking a question, instead of pleading my innocence.

"Uh-huh. Pick up that mess, please." He nods at the boxes. "And after that, head over to the Mech Shop and check on my upgrade. I get the feeling you need something to keep you busy."

I grumble. "Fine."

I fix the boxes and files, then send Vee a message on my Link. *New info,* the message says, *on my way to Scissor's. Meet me if you can,* and then I head out.

SIX

VEE FINDS ME a few blocks from the Mech Shop. I fill her in on what I overheard.

"What kind of facility?" she asks.

"That's just it, I don't know. They didn't say."

"Hmm." She scratches the back of her head. She changed her hair since last I saw her. Now it's wound tight into a bun. "Maybe it's a robot production factory? Maybe that's why Ratch had ten thousand ThinkChips shipped in?"

"Could be, except . . . why would they need four people to access the place? The president of the UD being one of them? I'm not sure that makes sense. Old New York has been making bots for a while. Why would they need a locked-down facility for that?"

She nods. "You're right."

Someone across the street calls out to Vee. She waves hello and we keep walking.

"I bet Po knows," she says.

I snort. "Probably. Because he knows everything and I know nothing."

"So why don't you ask him?"

We round the next corner, and pass a clothing shop where a bunch of people are ogling the latest neon-implanted clothes. There's a picture hanging up in the front window of Po wearing the blue shirt. A blond girl points at him and nudges her friend. "Jam, St. Kroix is *sooooo* nuclear."

Vee slows and stares at the poster.

"Can you believe that?" I say.

"I can, actually. Your brother is kinda cute."

I roll my eyes. "Not you too!"

She hooks her arm around my neck. "Oh come on, FishKid. Someday that'll be you, and there will be someone rolling their eyes at you too."

"Doubt it."

We wait for a clear traffic signal and cross the next intersection. "So, anyway, your brother. Do you want me to talk to him? I could tell him I'm worried about my dad or something."

"No." I sigh. "I'll ask him." I had already tried, anyway. I'd just geared out before I could. Now I had even more questions, so maybe it was a good thing I'd

48

waited. I could bombard him with everything all at once.

"Are you sure?" Vee asks.

"Yeah. If Po has secrets, he's more likely to tell me than you. No offense."

She shrugs and hurries ahead of me. "Hard to offend me, bolt-head."

We only make it two feet inside the Mech Shop before Scissor's audience track starts up and lets out a big *woooohoo!*

Scissor has thousands of audio tracks—laughing and booing and ahhhhing—uploaded onto her system, and she adds the sound effects to almost any situation. It's like living in a TV studio with a live audience.

Sometimes it's really, really annoying. But I can't imagine Scissor being Scissor without her sound effects.

"So glad to see you, Trout!" Scissor shouts as her arms detach from her torso and grow five feet, wrapping me in a big snake hug.

Vee chuckles beside me.

"Scissor," I groan. "Please put your arms away."

"Oh, all right." She lets me go and her arms wave in the air for a second, like the tentacles on an octopus, before she sucks them back inside her torso. "So, to what do I owe the pleasure of your faces today?"

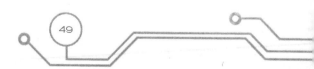

"Dad wanted me to check on his upgrade. And he used that as an excuse to get me out of command center."

"Awwww," the audience says.

Scissor's front panel—made of an LED screen—flashes a sad face. "I'm sorry to hear that, Trout. But I promise I will try to be good company. Perhaps I can't make up for the excitement you would surely be witnessing in command center, but I do have something that might match it very nearly."

Vee and I share a look. "What is it?" Vee asks.

Scissor grins real big. "Follow me and you'll see!"

She leads us into the back room. The place is so packed with parts and tools that it's hard to pick out anything of interest. The back wall is nothing but metal shelves stocked with old filters and robot joints and stacked gears. The counter in the center of the room is a tangle of twisted metal pieces and rubber-coated wires.

I have to step around an empty robot torso to get inside the room, and then nearly topple over a tower of robot manuals.

Scissor nods at the center table. "This is what I wanted to show you. I'm calling it the arthropod."

At first I think she's referring to the mess of parts on the table, but when I get closer, I see that she's point-

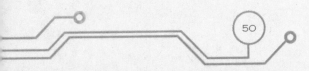

ing at a cage-like contraption the size of a human arm.

It's made up of several thin pieces of steel, welded together in a shape that reminds me of some of the exo-skeleton suits I see in vid games. The arm tapers off to a wrist, and then finally a glove.

Scissor plucks it off the table and turns it over. In the center of the hand is a circular object with folded claws and a clear lens. When Scissor presses a button, the lens glows neon blue, like the hover rails.

"Is that what I think it is?" Vee asks.

I glance over at her. "What do you think it is? I'm confused."

"It's armor," Scissor says, and her LED panel lights up bright pink, which usually means she's proud of herself. "It's also similar to my hoversuits, except this contraption creates its own hoverpoints."

"You don't need the rails?" I say, and the audience claps.

As it is now, most cars and hoverboards can't travel outside the rails. You need the rails to create boost. Some of the newer cars are called off-roaders, and they create their own boost, but they're super-expensive.

Scissor turns the arthropod away from us and points the palm at a stretch of brick wall in her shop. "Watch," she says, as if we would do anything else at this point.

She presses another button on the contraption's wrist and the glowing claw-like object in the center of the palm flies out with a heavy *whomp*.

The claws spread out and attach themselves to the brick. With another press of the button, the claws detach, and the object is sucked back into the arthropod.

"Whoa," Vee and I breathe as Scissor turns to me.

"Here, try it," she says.

"Me?"

She undoes a latch and the arm folds open. "Slide into it. Come on. It won't bite."

Hesitantly, I put my arm in, sliding my fingers into place. Scissor closes the piece and latches it.

"Now," she instructs, and guides me into position, squaring my shoulders. "Here's the button you press to shoot the hoverpoint." She gestures to a button on the inside of my thumb. "Press it again to retract it. Got it? Okay, now run and point it at the ceiling."

"What?" I croak.

"The hoverspot will catch you. No need to worry!"

Scissor is a genius when it comes to inventions, but testing out a brand-new creation by trying to hang myself from the ceiling? I don't know about that.

"If you won't, I will," Vee says, which means now I *have* to unless I want to look like a baby.

I stretch my fingers, like I'm testing the strength of the contraption. The steel moves silently at every joint.

Here goes nothing. I run, press the button, and point the glove toward the ceiling.

The claw shoots from the palm of my hand, and latches itself onto the ceiling fifteen feet away from me. I can feel its energy output on my skin, like static electricity. And once the two points—the one in the palm of my hand, and the claw object in the ceiling—sense each other, it's like they're made of magnets, and I get sucked in so that I'm hanging there in midair, about a foot of space between me and the claw.

"That is so wrenched!" Vee shouts. Scissor's audience track whistles.

"Now what?" I say.

"We leave you there," Vee answers.

"Very funny."

"Oh you two," Scissor clucks. "Press the button like I showed you."

I slide my thumb down the inside of the arthropod and push the button. When I do, the points deactivate and then I'm sailing for the ground. I hit hard, and pain shoots up both legs. I bury the cringe to hide it from Vee. At least I landed on my feet, which is more than I can say for the million other times I've fallen. Like the one time I found myself in a willow tree in Line Zero's park. I fell flat on my back, and knocked the wind from my lungs.

That wasn't fun.

And no one has let me forget about it.

"So, are they ready for the big time?" Vee asks as she turns my arm over in her hands to get a better look at the contraption. "When can I have one?"

"Give me a few more days." Scissor unlatches the arm and carefully sets it aside. "I guess that means you like it? Do you think it will be successful?"

Vee and I nod real hard. "Oh yeah. Mega successful," I answer.

Scissor beams. Her audience cheers.

I look around the workroom. "So, where is my dad's upgrade?"

Scissor snaps her fingers. "Right. This way!" She bustles over to one of the small worktables in the front of the shop. "Here it is. I'm calling it the Raven Blaster."

"Wow," I whisper.

The arm is propped up on two metal stands. It's the same size as Dad's current arm, but this is *definitely* an upgrade. The metal that makes up his joints and bones is thicker and darker, and I wonder if that automatically makes it stronger. There are orange lights running

through everything, so that it almost looks like veins. Small plates of metal make up the fingers, and it reminds me of the armor knights used to wear.

"That is so cracked," Vee says. "The good kind of cracked."

Scissor gently takes the arm from the stand. "It's made of carbonite neutro steel, so it's incredibly light, but stronger than almost any material out there. Here, feel it."

Scissor hands it to me and instantly I panic. What if I drop it? But I take it from her and I'm shocked at how light it is. It's no heavier than a donut.

"And you see the orange light?" Scissor asks. Vee and I nod. "That's a new weapon I'm working on. It's a Raven Blast. If anyone gets too close to your dad, all he has to do is hit a button and it'll send out a blast."

"Can I get one of those?" Vee asks with a grin.

I elbow her. "You were the one who just gave me a hard time about wanting a robotic limb!"

"That was before they made them with Raven Blasts!"

"Children! Children," Scissor says. "This is the only one of its kind in existence, so no, you can't have one. Besides, both of your fathers would kill me."

Vee deflates.

"Tell your dad it will be ready for him tomorrow," Scissor continues. "And if no other major projects come in, I will put a rush on the arthropods for you two. How does that sound?"

I grin. "That sounds wrenched."

Vee raises her brow. "And we get the first models, right?"

"Yes. I swear on my operating system, you will have the first that are available. Now go on! Let me get to work!"

We wave good-bye as she shoos us out of the store.

SEVEN

WHEN I GET back to the Fort, I check in with the house's new system to see where Po is. It tells me he's busy with Dad in command center, so I vow to corner him later and head into my room.

With nothing better to do, I cue up my newest vid game, Electro Race, and zone out for the next hour as I try to defeat King Primo. I'm *this close* to winning when my Link beeps. I look away from the TV for a second. Just long enough to get smashed by Primo.

Groaning, I drop the game controller and pick up my Link.

It's Tellie.

Suddenly, losing doesn't seem like such a big deal.

"Hey Tells," I answer.

"Hi, Goldfish," she says, calling me by the nickname she came up with when I lived in Brack.

Seeing her on my Link screen makes my stomach flip upside down, like I'm on a roller coaster. I'm glad to see her.

It's been over a week since we last talked, but this time, I know it'll be different.

Her dad was one of the people my dad mentioned with a code to the secret facility. And even though I know nothing *about* the facility, I can bet having a code isn't a good thing. At least not for Mr. Rix.

Dad said he'd have his people look out for Mr. Rix, but it still makes me nervous, for him and Tellie. Mostly Tellie, I remind myself, since it was her dad who attacked Po back before we left the UD. I saw him punch Po right before he handed him over to the UD government so they could hold him hostage.

I don't care how much I like Tellie. Secretly, I hate her dad. And I don't trust him.

"Whatchya been up to?" I ask as I sit in the window seat, one leg propped up on the cushion.

Tellie shrugs and straightens a blond curl between her pointer and middle finger. When she gets to the end of the lock of hair, she lets it go, and it springs into a curl again. "Nothing really."

Tellie and I went to the same school our entire lives and were never friends. Until I asked her to help me

make a vid to try to spread the word about my dad, back when he was missing after the Bot Wars ended.

She said yes right away.

Thankfully, she had a vid camera and a vid account. Tellie has everything anyone could ever want. But the more I get to know Tellie, the more I realize you can have everything you'd ever want and still have nothing that makes you happy.

"How are things in Brack?" I ask.

"The same. As always." She sighs.

"Is something wrong?" I ask. She's acting weird, and I start to wonder if maybe she knows whatever secret surrounds her dad.

Tellie tilts her head up and scrunches the bridge of her nose. "Can I tell you something? Something that you can't tell anyone?"

She *does* know! I swallow real hard. "Yeah, sure."

"Okay, well . . ." She straightens.

I lean closer to the Link. My heart thumps against my ribs.

"Ever since I helped you make that vid and you ran away with a robot and helped save your dad and your brother, I've just felt . . ." She trails off and looks to the right, away from the camera.

This isn't what I thought she was going to say.

59

"I've felt like the lamest person in the entire uni-verse," she finishes.

I can feel my eyebrows sinking lower on my face. "Wait. What?"

"You've done all these great things! And what have I done? Painted my nails a different color every day for three weeks straight? Which, yes, *is* a major feat, but still not life-changing—"

She doesn't know. My shoulders sink with relief. I didn't realize until now how badly I didn't want to see her sad about her father.

"—and I totally realize I'm whining. Because, *hello,* your dad was missing for, like, ever, and then when you finally found him, you found only half of him. So I probably shouldn't complain, but I haven't done any-thing important." She finally stops talking long enough to take a breath and look at me. "I haven't done any-thing important like you, Trout."

I drop my foot to the floor and turn, propping my elbows on my knees. "You know what's funny, though, is even though I've done all those things, and helped save a bunch of people, no one looks at me any differently." I hang my head. "Everyone here loves Po. I'm just a joke."

Tellie softens her voice. "Not to me, Goldfish."

That makes me smile.

"And speaking of your brother," she says, "did you hear the news yet?"

I sit upright. "No. What news?"

"He's giving my mom an exclusive interview."

"What?" I shout. "Since when?"

"His people confirmed this morning."

I snort. "Since when does he have *people*?"

Tellie shrugs. "How should I know? That's just what my mom said."

Po's "people" are probably Jules and Cole. They are the ones in charge of all incoming UD calls.

"When is this happening?"

"This week. My mom is dying to get him on air. *Everyone* has been dying to get an interview with him. You should see the girls at school. They all have Po backgrounds on their Links, and animated posters on their bedroom walls. It's kinda gross how much they love him."

I grumble to myself. *Gross* is probably the way I'd describe it too. "Where are they doing the interview?"

"Dekker's house."

Dekker, Aaron Dekker, is a Net star, and also one of Dad's contacts in Texas. His house, an old fire station in Edge Flats, is a safe house for people traveling between the UD and Bot Territory.

"Are you going?" I ask.

Tellie smiles, and I think I see her cheeks turn red. "I guess I can, if you want me to."

"We could hang out while they do the interview. It could be fun."

She nods. "All right. I'll ask my mom tonight." She pulls her hair back, off her shoulders, except for one strand that she winds around her finger again. "I guess I should go. I'm supposed to meet my friends later."

"All right. Have fun."

She smiles. "Bye, Goldfish."

I wave all nonchalantly before I hang up. That's how Po would do it.

When the connection ends, I stare at my Link background. It's still the same picture of a wolf monkey, but it reminds me of what Tellie said, about the girls at my old school putting pictures of Po on their Links.

Maybe, if I was wrenched like Po, Dad would finally let me in on his secret Meta-Rise meetings. Maybe he'd trust me more with the important stuff.

Maybe.

I just don't know how to make people look at me differently.

EIGHT

THE NEXT MORNING, the kitchen is bustling with activity. Dad sits across from me at the dining table downing a can of Life Water while Merril cooks breakfast for all the people showing up for work in command center.

Merril, who likes cooking special meals for any reason, no matter how small or special, is making raspberry pancakes this morning for Jules's birthday. I like pancakes, but not with raspberries, so I opt out and settle on Super Loopers cereal instead.

I fill my bowl to the brim, then drown the Loopers in milk. I take my first bite. Dad finishes off his Life Water and crushes the can in his robotic hand. Sometimes I wonder if he ever misses real food. I remember, when I was younger, he used to grill out every Sunday night for us. His favorite was barbequed ribs. Suddenly, I miss them too, and wonder if

I can talk Merril into barbequing for us sometime.

"I get my upgrade today," Dad says to me. "You want to come to Scissor's with me?"

I shrug. "Maybe."

"What did you think of it, when you saw it?"

"The Raven Blast is pretty cool."

Dad nods. "It's just added protection. I don't plan on using it."

"Then I hope you have a safety switch on that thing," I say, and laugh.

He grins. "Of course I do."

I start to say something about accidental Raven Blasts, when the house's alarm system starts blaring.

Some of the kids shriek, and run to their parents. The sound is deafening, like a foghorn in your ear.

Dad leaps to his feet.

I look over my shoulder at the news feed, but it's just a black screen. That's not a good sign. The news feed is always playing. Doesn't matter what time of the day or night it is.

Merril howls from the kitchen. The burners on the stove are blasting flames so high, they're scorching the shelves above.

"Parker! Fire extinguisher!" Dad says, but Parker is already moving.

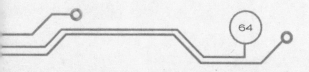

Vee ushers the kids out of the room. Po grabs a second fire extinguisher from the hallway and hurries past me into the kitchen.

Together, he and Parker put the fire out, covering the stove in thick white foam from the extinguishers.

When the chaos dies down, and we're sure everyone is safe, the Fort is silent save for the far-off whining of the kids in the entertainment room. They're scared, and so am I. Fact is, it could have been worse than just a burnt shelf.

"What the heck just happened?" Vee finally says.

The news feed is still black.

"Cole?" Dad says.

Cole starts for the elevator. "Already on it."

"You all right?" Dad asks me, and ruffles my hair like he used to when I was a kid.

"I'm fine."

He shakes his head. "I hate to think what could have happened if you were at the stove cooking, if no one had been around." His eyes get this far-off look and he scrubs at his face with his human hand. "Just glad no one was hurt."

"What could have caused that?" I ask, this sinking feeling in my gut.

Dad shakes his head. "I don't know. Faulty gas lines?"

I gesture to the blank news feed. "What about that?"

"Good question, son. I don't know."

We learn, not long after the fire, that it wasn't just our building that had issues. And the sick feeling in my stomach quadruples.

Before we have any information on the fire, before Dad will say anything about his theory, I know right away what caused it. Or *who* caused it. Ratch.

He threatened to hurt Dad, and now he did. He attacked Dad where it'd hurt the most—in the town he calls home.

All of the streetlights in Line Zero went crazy, causing traffic accidents all over the city. The lights in the public library shut off, and panic spread through the building. A TV exploded two houses down from us. The hover rails between Lawrence Street and Miller Avenue flickered out, leaving hundreds of people stranded.

Lots of public places were shut down. School was canceled for the week (which wasn't such a big deal, since we only had one day left anyway).

The problems were only in Line Zero, thankfully, but that just made Dad more anxious.

Vee and I go upstairs to command center, to see if Cole has uncovered any information.

And that's where we are when the news feed flickers out again, and the room goes deadly still. We all tense up, on alert.

It only takes a second for the screen to come to life, but it isn't the UD feed that comes on. It's just a blank brick wall, and sitting in front of it is Ratch.

Dread knots around my chest till I feel like I can't breathe. There was a time, not that long ago, when I looked up to Ratch. When I thought he was mega cool. Now the very thought of him makes the hair on my neck stand up.

"Hello, Robert," Ratch says. Dad crosses his arms in front of him. Since the footage is broadcasting across the news feed, and not through a Link, Ratch can't see Dad, and he can't hear what's going on in command center, but something tells me he knows Dad well enough to have a mental picture of what's going on. That Dad looks like he's doing everything in his control not to start yelling and cursing. That LT looks defeated and lost because Ratch was his best friend and he deceived LT when it mattered most. That Parker and Jules and Cole are tapping away at their computers, doing what they do best: Looking for leads on Ratch's whereabouts, trying to trace the signal he's using to broadcast.

Mostly, though, I'm thankful Ratch can't see me,

because if he could, he'd notice right away how geared out I am. I can feel the blood draining from my face, the fear pooling in my gut. Every nerve in my body is screaming at me to run. Ratch could be thousands of miles away, but I'm still worried that he somehow has the ability to reach through the screen, grab me by the neck, and shake me till I'm nothing but space dust.

But then, Ratch tilts his head just slightly, and I get a flash of him holding his friend Mel in his arms, in the middle of some factory back before the Bot Wars, and the fear transforms into sadness.

"As I'm sure you know by now, Line Zero, at large, was attacked. I'm calling it digital warfare. I rather like the label. It sounds . . . innovative."

Dad shifts and Po moves closer to him, like a second in command. Parker used to be Dad's second before Po came here. But the more time goes on, the more Po seems to be taking over that position.

"As with any attack, there is a motive," Ratch says. "I want Robert St. Kroix to step down as the leader of the Meta-Rise. I want him to name LT as his successor . . ."

Command center grows loud with murmurs and gasps, but my dad quiets them with the wave of his hand.

"The Meta-Rise stands for justice," Ratch says, "but

not for humans, for robots, and it shouldn't be led by a human.

"Only a robot can understand the plight of another robot.

"That attack on Line Zero could have been avoided, if the so-called leader of the largest group in the city focused on the issues that really mattered. Freedom. Power. Strength. Bot Territory will perish if it continues to pretend that peace is possible. Because it's not. What Bot Territory needs to do is prepare itself for another war. It's coming, whether we like it or not. The United Districts will never accept who we are, and who we've become, and the sooner we band together—we as in the *machine* race—the more likely we are to be the victors."

Ratch stands up, so all we can see is his torso. His arms reach for something out of frame. A second later, the camera shifts and tilts upward, and Ratch stares down at all of us through the lens, his band of orange eyes glinting.

"Step down, Robert St. Kroix," he says, "or my next attack will be bigger than a few defunct stoplights and gas burners."

The screen flickers and cuts out. A long drawn-out beeping noise fills the room, followed by complete silence. No one stands up to support Dad, to show him

they still have his back. Instead, they stare at him out of the corners of their eyes, like they're waiting for him to say something to show he's unafraid.

But he doesn't. Instead, he turns around and heads straight for the elevator. It takes me a second to realize what he's doing, and I race after him.

"Dad! Dad!"

He stops at the doors and presses the button.

"You aren't going to listen to Ratch, are you?" I ask.

Dad rocks back on the heels of his boots as he waits. "I don't know, son."

"It'd be dumb to step down. You created the Meta-Rise. It wouldn't be what it is today without—"

"He's right, though, isn't he?" Dad hunches, like all the fight has drained out of him. "The Meta-Rise represents robots more than anything else. Humans don't need someone to speak out for them. They aren't the victims here. Maybe a robot *should* lead the Meta-Rise."

"But you're human *and* robot. No one understands both sides better than you."

The elevator doors slide open and Dad steps inside without saying another word.

The doors close, leaving me standing there in command center, even more confused and frustrated than I was before.

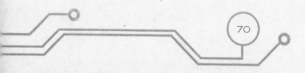

NINE

I DON'T SEE DAD much the next day. No one does. It isn't that he's busy, wrapped up in his work, it's that he's been absent from everything. From the breakfast table, from command center. LT says Dad is sick, but I think he knows I know that's a lie. Dad has been hiding, and it's because of what Ratch said.

I never thought I'd see the day when my dad let someone shake him up like that.

The day after Ratch's digital attack, the UD puts Mr. Rix on the news feed with an *Important Announcement*.

Vee and I are in my bedroom playing a vid game when the announcement comes on. According to the emblem on the podium box Mr. Rix stands behind, he's at the UD's capitol in 2nd District. The emblem is of an eagle with six stars positioned around it. A 3-D image of the UD flag billows in the nonexistent wind just over his shoulder.

He's dressed in a serious black suit with pointy gold shoulder pads. His graying hair is slicked over. Even though he's acting the part of a polished and powerful congressman, something about him is all wrong. There are dark half-circles beneath his eyes, and wrinkles on his forehead. He's paler than normal, which I guess isn't a big deal—maybe he just stopped doing that fake tan stuff—but for someone like Mr. Rix, I think it means something important. "As I'm sure you have all heard by now," Rix says, "there was an attack on Line Zero, in Bot Territory, yesterday morning. The attack seemed to be aimed at causing mayhem on various electronics and household appliances. Thankfully, no one was hurt, but it could have been so much worse."

Rix takes a breath and runs a hand over his tie, smoothing it down. His eyes sweep across whatever, or whoever, is behind the camera. He fidgets with the paper on the podium before speaking again. "We don't want to alarm anyone, but there is no telling what else a malevolent robot might do. And if this robot group is turning against their own kind, just think of what they'll do to us."

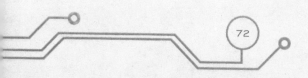

"It's not that Ratch has turned against us," Vee says. "It's that he's gone totally nuclear."

"Technological warfare is the future of terrorism," Mr. Rix goes on. "I think it's time we come to terms with that fact. We've evolved into a race that relies too much on technology, and robots will exploit that. It wasn't too long ago when we relied on them, and look where it's gotten us.

"In light of the recent attacks, the UD has every reason to believe it may be next. In order to protect our country, we've had our top-notch tech team doing everything they can to strengthen our technological infrastructure. We assure you, you are safe here in the UD, but please, do not associate with anyone in Bot Territory. Every link to there creates a possible breach point in our security. Robots are, and always will be, our enemies."

Rix takes a breath, presses his dry lips together as he stares into the camera. It's like he's looking straight at me. "Stay alert. Stay informed. Stay United. Not everything is as it seems these days. The more we know, the safer we are."

The broadcast cuts out and the regular news feed starts up again.

Vee tosses her game controller aside. "I call horse crap. Robots are not our enemy. Funny thing is, if the UD knew the truth about the Robot Wars, none of this would be happening right now."

I grab my soda off the nightstand. "You think?"

"Yup." She walks to the window and looks out over the street below. Her hair turns golden for a second. "If the UD people knew the real truth about robots, that they're not all bad, that they just want to be treated fairly, then a lot more people would support the UD and Bot Territory coming together again, instead of separating us with the border."

They're not all bad . . .

Her words echo in my head.

"What makes a robot bad, you think?" I ask.

She shrugs and turns around to face me. The setting sun casts a halo of light around her head. "I don't know, FishKid. I've never really thought about it."

I take a swig of my soda and set it down. "Well, I have. I've thought about it a lot."

Vee frowns. "This is about Ratch, isn't it?" I don't say anything, which I guess tells her enough. "You wonder why Ratch turned on us?"

"Yeah. I do. And what if LT turns on us in the future? Or Scissor? Why is Ratch different?"

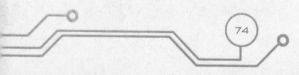

"Because . . ." She throws her arms up. "He's evil! Humans can be evil too!"

"Robots aren't humans."

"That's bog and you know it. If LT heard you say that, he'd be giving you a lecture right now."

"Well, they're not! Their emotions are programmed into them, aren't they? That's what the ThinkChip is. Just a computer chip with computer programming and—"

She crosses her arms in front of her. "And you're starting to sound like the UD government's propaganda brochures!"

I can tell she's getting mad, but I can't seem to stop myself from plowing forward.

"Maybe they're not all wrong! How can we know for sure LT won't turn on us? I liked Ratch a few months ago. I thought he was totally wrenched!"

"I could turn on you tomorrow. I could tell all the kids at school about that time you ate dog food because you thought they were fig cookies."

"They looked like cookies!"

"Or about how you cried at the end of *Save the Panda*—"

"It was a sad movie!"

She cocks out her hip. "My point is, anyone can turn

on anyone at any time, for a number of reasons. There are no guarantees!"

I snort. "I would never turn on my dad, or Po. That's a guarantee. And that's because we share blood. Families don't turn on each other."

Vee pulls back like I just slapped her. Instantly I can tell I've crossed a line I didn't know was there.

"Vee?" I say quietly.

She blinks and a tear streams down her face. She swipes it away quickly. "Then tell me, Trout, why would a mother, a *human* mother, leave her daughter? Huh? What's the reason for that? We share blood. She made me. If what you say is true, then she should have loved me forever, unconditionally. Families aren't supposed to turn on each other, according to you. That's what makes us better than robots."

"Vee, that's not what I meant. I mean . . ."

"Then what did you mean?"

"I . . ."

"Exactly." She shakes her head. "You know what? Besides my dad, the only family I've had, who stuck around and took care of me, were robots. No one is perfect. Love isn't in the blood we share with other humans. Because if it was, my mom would have never left me."

With that, she turns around and stomps out of my room.

I think about running after her and apologizing and telling her I was wrong, but truth is, I'm too embarrassed to do it.

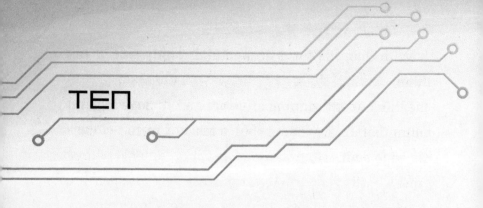

TEN

VEE AVOIDS ME for the next two days, so when the September Festival rolls around, I consider not going. I wanted to go with her. Without Vee, I've got no one. All of my new friends are people I met through her, which means they're either not my real friends (at least not yet) or that she'll be hanging out with them at the festival instead of me. And what if she yells at me again? Or tells everyone what I said?

I've been feeling the shame of the things I've said to her for two days. I don't want to start all over again.

Po finally talks me into going to the festival by promising me a funnel shake, which is this chocolaty ice cream drink with a cake funnel in the middle. It's the best, after Bot-N-Bolts ice cream, that is, and it's hard for me to say no to it.

The September Festival is held at the fair grounds north of Line Zero. Po drives us there and Marsi lets me

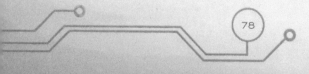

have the front seat, which I think is pretty nice of her. After parking, we make our way to the main part of the fair. At the entrance, several food carts line the thoroughfare. A woman with a head of giant red curls shouts about salted caramel peanuts. Smoke billows from a grill where turkey legs roast over an open fire. A bot with a tiny head but big arms sells broccoli pops that he promises taste like cotton candy.

The farther inside the festival we get, the bigger it feels. It's like there are miles and miles of spinning, flashing carnival rides, and aisles and aisles of games. There's Laser Shot, Alien Invasion, Toss a Ring & Win a Link, and Holo Jump. Each game is surrounded by three walls stuffed full of prizes. I try to beg a few creds out of Po to play Laser Shot, but he tells me to buzz off.

It doesn't take me long to find the shake stand. I race to get in line, and bounce on my feet as Po and Marsi catch up. The digital sign at the top of the stand advertises new flavors. Raspberry ice cream with cheesecake. Chocolate ice cream with strawberry cake.

The strawberry one sounds good, but I'm going for the original. Po and Marsi pick the new raspberry one.

While we're walking around, eating our funnel shakes, Po is stopped by a group of kids. The girls hang around the edges of the group, whispering and giggling, while the boys ask Po about Ratch, and Dad, and what it was like to fight in the Bot Wars.

He gives Marsi and me an apologetic look, but Marsi just waves to him, and tells him to take his time.

"How come you're not bothered by all of the attention Po gets?" I ask Marsi as we saunter away.

"Why would it bother me?"

I shrug. "I don't know."

"Are *you* bothered by it?"

I don't say anything at first, then everything comes pouring out. "They're interviewing him for a TV show. Like he's a celebrity or something. I mean . . . all he did was give a speech after the attack on Edge Flats."

Marsi laughs, and it isn't until now that I realize her laugh is like a wind chime and a baby giggle put together. No wonder Po likes her so much. Making her laugh somehow makes me feel like top gear. Like I've just done something super-special.

"Now it all makes sense," she says.

"What?"

"You think Po likes the attention?"

"Doesn't he?"

"Well . . ." She takes a spoonful of her shake before answering. "I think in some ways, he likes it. Remember what he was like in Brack?"

I do. He worked a lot so he could pay the bills and buy me vid games and put food in the fridge. He wasn't happy. I know that much. Or at least, deep down he wasn't. He tried to act like everything was fine.

"Po feels bad, you know," Marsi goes on. "I mean, he feels bad for you. Whenever someone brings up saving Edge Flats, he makes sure he mentions you. You're the reason Edge Flats survived. He knows that. He wants to make sure you're given credit."

My face warms. "Really?"

"Yes."

"Why wouldn't he tell me that?"

"Because he knows you'd never believe him."

That's probably true.

"Yeah," I say as we pass a glowing vending machine, "but he still gets special treatment from my dad. And he knows all the important stuff. I don't get to be at any of the Meta-Rise meetings."

"Have you ever considered that it's your father who wants it that way? Not your brother?"

"Well . . . yeah . . ."

"All I'm saying is, cut him some slack. He really doesn't like the whole celebrity bit. I promise."

We head for a road off the main thoroughfare where tents and exhibits are set up on either side. There's a

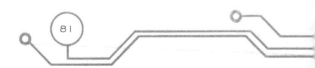

tent with a man carving animals out of logs with a laser saw, and a tent selling handmade jewelry. There's an exhibit of concept cars, and hydro vegetables and hybrid animals. There's even a woman claiming to be a psychic.

She shouts to me as we walk by, the dozen silver bracelets on her wrist sliding down to her elbow as she waves. "Come, and I'll show you your future, dearie."

"No thanks," I say.

"Oh, but it's a good one! I can tell."

I follow Marsi closely, and look at the psychic over my shoulder. She's staring right at me.

She's not super-old, maybe like forty or something, and thin as an envelope with knobby elbows, and bony wrists.

When she smiles, I spot a gap between two teeth, where she must have lost one.

"It's a good one," she mouths again.

I glance at Marsi. Her back is to me as she flips through a rack of summer dresses.

I shuffle quietly away.

The psychic smiles as I near.

"I don't have any creds," I tell her, because I don't want her getting her hopes up.

"I don't either," she answers.

I frown, because I'm not sure what that's supposed to mean.

She winks and ducks down, putting us nearly face-to-face. I didn't realize until I was standing right in front of her how much taller she is than me. She looked so small a second ago.

"What's your name, boy?" she asks, her voice quiet and raspy. Her breath smells like peppermint and coffee.

I answer with a fake name. "Tom."

She smiles a knowing smile. "Tom, is it? Well, *Tom*, do you have a specific question for me? Something been bothering you lately?"

There are a dozen somethings lately, but I'm not sure where to start. And anyway, I'm not sure I believe in psychics. So it's not like I'm going to ask her something important and hope to get an answer.

After a beat, she leans closer. "Go on."

I blurt out the first question that comes to mind. "Will my dad be okay?"

She straightens to her full height. Behind her, over her shoulder, the Ferris wheel glows against the darkening sky. "Your dad will be as safe as he can be."

I frown again. "That's not really an answer."

"And that wasn't the right question."

I don't know what to say to that. I start to turn away,

because I think she might be making fun of me, and I don't want to lose Marsi in the crowd.

"None of us are ever safe," she says.

I turn back around.

"You will come into great power someday," she adds. "Then it will be up to you to keep your dad safe."

An arm snakes around my shoulders and I lurch back.

"It's just me," Marsi says, and looks from me to the psychic.

"Rise from the heap, Trout," the psychic says as Marsi pulls me away.

Po catches up to us a while later. "Jules just called me on my Link. Said we should head over to the grandstand. Dad is about to make an announcement."

My heart plummets to my knees. "What kind of announcement? Is it about Ratch's demand? About quitting the Meta-Rise?"

"No idea." Po hooks his arm around my neck and drags me toward the grandstands. "He doesn't tell me everything, ya know?"

I look at Marsi and she winks. "I know."

We find an open spot in the grandstand area that

overlooks a field that is used for monster-truck races, demolition derbies, and any other sport that calls for a mud pit. There's a dais at the edge of the field, before the pit, and that's where Dad is now.

Behind him, cars are lined up for the first leg of the demolition derby. Most of the cars are older models that were made before the hover rails, and even if they weren't, they were transformed back into fuel cars. There are no rails here.

I think for a second that Dad is going to open the derby, that he's going to say something about the festival, and about having fun, but as soon as he addresses the crowd, I can tell by the tone of his voice that his announcement isn't about the festival at all.

"Ladies, gentlemen, and robots, I'm glad you could make it to the September Festival."

The grandstand goes quiet save for the occasional yelp of a baby. Next to me, an older couple shushes each other, but continues to chomp loudly on their shared bucket of popcorn. Po stiffens on my other side, as if he's ready to spring into action should he be needed. Though I have no idea what they'd need him to do. Does he think Ratch is going to show up?

"We've been planning this event for weeks," Dad

continues, "and, despite what has been transpiring lately, you all showed up to support the effort put into the festival, and to show unity.

"For that, I thank you."

He takes a breath. "As many of you know, the recent attack on Line Zero was claimed by Ratch. Our friend in the past, who, for reasons unknown to us, has chosen a different path. In his recent broadcast to Bot Territory, and the UD, he asked that I forfeit my role as leader of the Meta-Rise."

Dad pauses, paces to one end of the dais, and looks up at the crowd. LT is there too, in the middle of the stage, hands folded in front of him. Parker is there, along with Jules and Cole.

My stomach knots.

"I'm here today," Dad says, and he looks across the dais at LT, "to tell you that I will not, under any circumstances, kneel down to the demands of a rogue robot bent on causing destruction to humans and robots alike."

The crowd roars around us. People are on their feet, clapping and whistling and shouting.

"I made a promise to the citizens of Line Zero, and more than that, the citizens of Bot Territory, to stand up for them. Whether they were human or robot. I do

not see a distinguishing line between both species. We are all citizens here. And there is no one better than me, a half man, half robot, to lead them. I understand the plight of both sides.

"And I will do everything in my power to make them one."

He raises his fist in the air. Everyone in the grandstands is now up, and they raise their fists too. I stand on the bench to see better.

"Rise from the heap!" Dad shouts, and everyone around me echoes the Meta-Rise motto.

For 2.5 seconds, as Dad exits the stage, I'm happy he didn't surrender his position. I'm proud of him. I feel the energy from the crowd raising the hair on my arms and the back of my neck, and I think everything is all right.

But then I think of Ratch seeing this broadcast, and I think of what he might do when he realizes my dad didn't do as he asked.

And I know it won't be good.

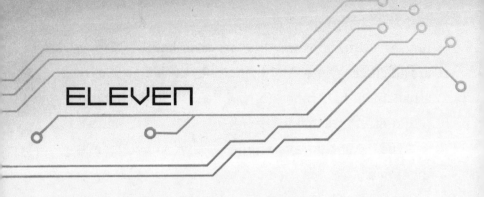

ELEVEN

THE FORT SPENDS the rest of the night celebrating, even after the festival shuts down. Vee doesn't show, which proves even more how long she can hold a grudge, and how big that grudge must be against me. She must hate me.

When I wake up the next morning after just a few hours of sleep, I feel like I got run over by a bus. Worse yet, I'm supposed to see Tellie today, during Po's interview with her mom, and I don't even feel like crawling out of bed.

Somehow, I make it, and shower and eat breakfast. Just after noon, we're on our way to Edge Flats, Texas, to Dekker's house.

Po elbows me, and since we're in the darkened maintenance tunnels, and I didn't see the jab coming, I

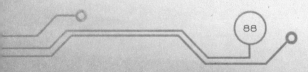

stumble from the blow and knock into one of the dozen or so pipes lining the tunnel wall. A loud clang echoes around us.

"Shhhh!" Po says, and laughs.

"You're not very funny!"

Marsi comes to my side and hands me one of the portable glow lamps. "Here. Take mine."

"Are you sure?"

She smiles and nods. "Of course I'm sure."

"Thanks," I say, and take the offering.

Po snorts. "Do you want me to hold your weetle hand, Trout?"

"Shut up."

"Boys," Dad says ahead of us. "Stop harassing each other."

LT hangs back and walks with me. "Are you all right?"

"I'm fine."

"You do not sound fine. I detect a melancholy thread in the tone of your voice."

"I said I was fine."

"Does this have anything to do with the fact that Vee would not come with us to Texas? Did you two have a disagreement?"

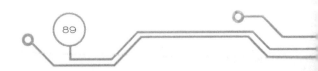

The tunnel veers to the left.

Technically that's not it. Technically I'm gearing out about Dad's announcement and Ratch's reaction, but I think LT is the last person I can tell. He was Ratch's best friend once. I know it's hard for him to hear anything bad about Ratch.

So I don't say anything and let LT think it's Vee I'm upset about. I guess I still am anyway. So it's not a total lie.

"I see," he finally says after my long drawn-out silence.

"What does that mean?" I look over at him, my light illuminating his face. "Like, *I see,* as in you're not surprised? Or *I see,* as in she said something about me and now it's all making sense?"

"Neither, though it does all make sense now."

"You're confusing me."

He doesn't elaborate. "What was the disagreement about?"

"Ummm . . . well . . ." My stomach churns. I can't tell him that we argued about robots, about whether or not they can feel emotion. It makes me feel like a loser.

"Nothing big," I answer.

"Mm-hmm. Well, if you want to talk about it, I am here. You know that."

"Yeah," I say. "I do."

We make it to our exit and climb up the ladder to street level. We leave the tunnels behind for a quiet alley in the border town of Awaso. There's a car waiting for us. Or, rather, a giant SUV. Big enough to fit all six of us. It's a self-driving car, so we all climb into the main sitting compartment, which is basically like a U-shaped couch with several nav screens and a manual steering wheel at the front, just in case the self-driving system breaks down.

Dad keys in Dekker's address and the car takes off silently.

LT shifts next to me, and tilts his head, like he's listening to a frequency we can't hear. "It is Dekker," he says, which I take to mean Dekker has called LT's direct communication system. "Mrs. Rix has arrived along with hair and makeup—"

"Po is having makeup put on?" I burst out laughing. "I can't wait to see this."

Po punches me in the arm. "Everyone on TV gets makeup, you idiot."

"Ouch!"

"Po," Marsi says, and Po sits back.

Dad smirks. "Marsi, I must say, you are a welcome addition to this family."

"Yeah. Maybe we should ditch Po and adopt Marsi. I like her better anyway," I say.

"Ha. Ha." Po curls his upper lip at me.

We arrive at Dekker's in record speed. This model of car—the Panther—is top-notch, with an accelerated traveling system that can travel on and off the rails. I think I need one of these. I could go see Lox in the UD whenever I wanted.

I'm the first inside Dek's house, and hurry up the stairs, taking them two at a time. When I reach the upper level, and step out of the stairwell, a pillow is lobbed in my direction.

"Hey!"

The replying laughter—part wailing hyena, part snorting pig—is a familiar laugh that I'm happy to hear.

"Lox?" I shout, and lunge at my best friend, giving him a tackle hug, even though I know in most situations, it'd be totally lame. I don't care. I missed him. "What are you doing here?"

Lox pats me on the back. "You kidding? Can't keep me away!"

"Or maybe it's that I called him and asked if he wanted to come with."

I turn around at the sound of Tellie's voice. She's

smiling at me real big. Before I think about what I'm doing, or what it means, I'm hugging her too. She smells like caramel popcorn and cinnamon, like a carnival. She reminds me instantly of home, even though Brack isn't home anymore and probably never will be again.

"Nice to see you, Goldfish."

"Yeah. You too."

Lox claps. "Okay. Okay. Break it up!"

Footsteps thump down the stairs from the second floor. "Little dude!" Dekker calls when he sees me. His rainbow-dyed hair sticks out every which way, like a parrot with ruffled feathers.

"Hey Dek."

"Missed you, little dude." He reaches over and messes up my hair, so that it probably matches his. I don't bother fixing it.

"How ya been?" he asks.

I shrug. "Good. You know."

Dek tsks and looks at Dad as he comes up behind me. "His life is turned upside down, he rescues his brother from the clutches of the evil United Districts, and saves the world. And what's he say? 'Good.' Little dude has been good."

Dad chuckles. "That's a twelve-year-old for you."

"I'm almost thirteen."

"Yeah. Yeah." Po hooks me with his arm and gives me a bolt burn across the top of my head. "Thirteen in eleven days, three hours, four minutes, and twenty-five seconds. Right, Trout? You have a countdown on your Link so you don't forget."

"You guys all need your brains thawed."

That makes them laugh real hard.

High heels click across the floor toward us. Mrs. Rix, dressed in a bright green dress, enters the room. Eye makeup, the same green as her dress, swoops up toward her eyebrows. Glowing neon earrings dangle from her ears. I've only meet Mrs. Rix once in person before this, and she seems just as intimidating now as she did then. There's something about her that I don't like, but can't ignore either. Power is what Dad would probably call it. Like she can command every-one's attention with only the sound of her heels on the hardwood floor.

"Glad you could all make it," she says, in that clipped voice of hers, and everyone goes silent. "We're set up if Mason is ready."

We all look at Po. Mason is his real name, but hardly anyone ever calls him that.

"I'm ready," he says.

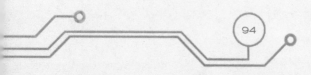

"Good." Mrs. Rix looks to Dek. "Dekker, dear, could you come double-check the feeds for me? This substitute crew is wretchedly incompetent."

I catch Tellie rolling her eyes behind her mom's back.

"Sure, Mrs. R.," Dekker says. "I'm on my way."

Mrs. Rix gestures to Po. "Follow me."

"Ma'am, can my girlfriend watch from behind the camera?"

Mrs. Rix waves her hand without even looking at Marsi. "Sure. As long as she's quiet during filming."

They disappear through the doorway at the back of the living room. It leads to the front of the fire station, to what was once the main office. Tellie, Lox, and I hurry to the doorway and peek through the window. There are two chairs facing each other, one for Po and one for Mrs. Rix. There are three cameras set up around the room, with studio lights rigged up all over the place so that it looks like a football field at night.

Po sits in his chair while a tiny girl powders his face.

"Will it be live?" I ask.

"Semi-live," Tellie answers. "Meaning, the footage will be delayed enough that if they need to edit something, they can. That's what that guy"—she nods at the bald guy in the back corner of the room—"is here for. He's in control of whatever goes on air."

I have to admit, even though this whole thing is for my brother, it is kinda wrenched. I never would have thought six months ago, when Po and I were living in Brack in our run-down house, that we'd someday be here, in Aaron Dekker's house, filming a TV show.

When Dek finishes checking the feeds, he makes his way toward us and we all scramble. He grins when he comes out into the living room. "Spying, were you?"

"Hardly," Tellie says at the same time Lox says, "Jam right!"

"I got a better idea," Dek says. "I have popcorn and a big screen up on the second floor. We can watch it as it airs."

Lox picks up a remote tab, probably for the TV down here, or maybe Dek's sound system. He starts tapping at the screen before Dek plucks it from his hands and sets it back down.

"Little hyper dude," Dek says, using the nickname he gave Lox, "no touch."

Not only is Lox always into stuff, Dek has obsessive compulsive disorder. Everything has its place, and Lox is notorious for putting things where they don't belong. Or worse, where they'll never be found.

"Got it, Captain," Lox says with a salute.

"Come on." I motion everyone toward the stairs.

"Sounds like they're about to start, and I don't want to miss anything."

Po's interview is scheduled to air at four p.m. By then, we're all settled in the spare bedroom, gathered around the big-screen TV. Tellie, Lox, and I pulled up chairs and set them in front of the TV. Dad and LT joined us a few minutes before 4:00 and went directly to the windows to whisper to each other about something I can't hear.

Dekker is lounged back on the bed, his arms propped behind his head. He's tossing handfuls of popcorn into his mouth, while talking around it. "You know, six months ago, no one even knew Po existed. That's fame for you. By this time next year, if Po plays his cards right, he'll be rich and famous, and a crowd will gather around him whenever he goes outside."

"Po is terrible at poker," Lox says.

"Not what I meant," Dekker says.

"But it's what I meant," Lox counters, which makes Tellie snort.

After a commercial break, the intro to *Getting to Know Brack* comes on and I shush everyone. Even Dad and LT stop whispering. A pre-filmed clip comes on where Mrs. Rix talks about Po and the St. Kroix family, and Po's rise to becoming a hero.

The footage cuts to Dekker's house, to Po sitting alongside Dekker's wall of found art. There's a display of vintage plates with geometric designs on them. A sign made out of old wood, with a painted quote that says *We're all mad here*. And a garbage can lid with one of the old presidents painted on it.

"Mason," Mrs. Rix says, "tell us, what's life like now, after what some are calling the Meta-Rise Freedom Speech?"

Po smiles, flashing ultra-white teeth. "Life is . . ." He trails off, and looks away from Mrs. Rix. He shrugs. "It's kila."

Mrs. Rix tilts her head. "That must mean it's good?"

Po chuckles. "It's really good. Better than ever."

"You have, by some accounts, become a celebrity. Would you agree?"

"I don't know about that. I'm still the same guy. I still eat Loopers for breakfast. I still work hard for what I have. I would still do anything for my family."

"And speaking of your family, as many know, you're the son of Robert St. Kroix, half man, half robot, the leader of the Meta-Rise. I've heard you dubbed as the prince of the revolution. Do you feel the pressure of that position?"

"Oh, for sure. Even though I don't feel like I am *that*

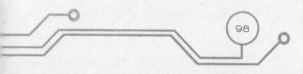

person, that I have any more power than the next guy. But I know people are looking at me to *be* that person. To stand up for those who have no voice. To do what's right for humans and robots—"

"And what *is* right?" Mrs. Rix asks. "What is the Meta-Rise's next step?"

"Come on, Mrs. Rix"—he flashes a secretive smile—"you know I can't talk about that kind of stuff."

Behind us, Dek chuckles. "And there goes the heart of every teenage girl in the universe."

"Do you always ask for your dad's permission?" Mrs. Rix continues.

Po gets this serious look on his face. "I do. When it comes to that kind of thing. I trust him. I trust his vision. He's a good man."

"What are your thoughts on Ratch's recent demand that your father step down as leader of the Meta-Rise?"

I feel like everyone in the room takes a deep breath and holds it.

"Well . . . I understand where Ratch is coming from, I think." Po pauses, then: "He wants to stand up for his kind, which is admirable, but I think he's doing robots a huge disservice by closing them off to evolution, and the advancement of our world."

"How so?"

"My dad will not be the first and only human with robot parts. It will become commonplace someday. And then the lines between humans and bots will blur. The UD hates robots, and Ratch hates humans, but to continue to segregate the two will only lead to disaster."

LT walks past us to the bedroom doorway and freezes, like he's listening for something. All robots have a better sense of hearing than humans, and LT's is one of the best. He can hear things for miles if he focuses hard enough.

"What is it?" Dad asks.

"Someone is here," LT says. "And I think I know who it is."

Dad tenses up. "Who?"

"Nathaniel Rix."

Tellie sits forward. "My dad is here?"

"Kids, stay here," Dad says, and he and LT jet from the room.

None of us are watching the broadcast anymore. I start for the door too, but Dekker stops me. "Little dude, wait."

"I want to know what's going on. If my dad is in trouble, I need to help him."

"My dad wouldn't be here to cause trouble," Tellie

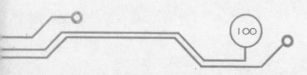

argues, and I want to tell her she doesn't know what she's talking about. But she doesn't know all of the terrible things her dad's done, and she might not believe me if I told her.

"There's another way to eavesdrop, if that's what you want to do," Dek says.

Lox sighs. "No respect for your elders, Trout. No respect."

"Shut up, Lox," Tellie and I say in unison.

Dekker pulls his Link out of his back pocket and taps in a few things. "I have an app for this. Have my house's entire security system programmed into it. And the system includes audio." He taps in one more thing and the audio starts playing.

"What are you doing here, Rix?" Dad says.

The app is only set on audio, so there's no picture, but I think Dad and LT are keeping Mr. Rix at the front door. From the sound of it, he's alone. "Something's happened and . . ." He pulls in a deep breath, and when he speaks next, his voice is shaking, like he's trying not to cry or gear out. "The president was kidnapped this morning. Disappeared from his private rooms. There has been no sign of him since, no ransom demands. Nothing and I'm . . ."

"You're worried you're next," Dad fills in.

Mr. Rix is silent for a second, then: "You know, don't you? About the facility in ONY?"

"I do," Dad says.

Tellie looks at me, her eyes narrowed. "What facility? What is going on, Trout?"

"I don't know . . . I mean . . ."

"This suddenly seems like a colossally bad idea," Dek mutters, and moves to disconnect the app.

I grab his wrist. "Just a few more seconds, please."

Mr. Rix starts talking again. "If you know, then you must also be aware of the fact that there are only two of us left, and I'm the next easiest target. Georgette has been off the grid for a long time . . . Ratch will most likely wait to take her last. And if he's able to kidnap the president, then I don't stand a chance."

There's jostling, a brush of fabric. "I need to see my wife and daughter. Please?"

Dad exhales. "Of course. They're upstairs. Will you tell them what's going on?"

"I can't." A door slams shut. "I just want to pretend I'm here to say hello, then I'm gone. I want to get as far away from them as I can. So they're safe."

I glance over at Tellie. For the last several months, she's been doing that fake tan stuff like her dad, but suddenly she looks like she's got the flu. She's paler

than normal, with a weird, unhealthy yellow tint to her cheeks.

"I'm sure there's an explanation," I say.

She shakes her head and starts for the door when LT appears. His eyes scan us, and somehow, using whatever magical robot powers he has, zeroes in on what we've done.

"Dekker," he says in a deep, gravelly voice. A voice that is very much not LT's voice. "What did you do?"

"Mmmm." Dek puts his Link away. "Nothing big."

"I want to see my dad," Tellie says, and squares her shoulders. Even though she's still wary of robots, she doesn't show any fear. Tellie's always been good at that kind of thing, of staying strong when it counts. Like my dad. And Po.

"Your father will be here momentarily," LT answers. "Please give him a moment to speak with your mother."

I glance at the TV, knowing Po's interview is supposed to be live, wondering how they'll manage to postpone the footage if Mr. Rix wants to see his wife. Maybe there will be extra commercials?

Tellie starts pacing the room, her arms crossed tightly in front of her. "This is ridiculous."

Getting to Know Brack comes back on the air. Mrs.

Rix is still interviewing Po, which must mean she isn't able to take a break yet.

Tellie stops pacing to watch the show with the rest of us. The sooner Mrs. Rix asks for a commercial break, the sooner Tellie will be able to see her dad.

We're all standing around waiting when a commotion sounds from behind the camera. Po leaps out of his chair. "Get my dad. Now!"

Someone shrieks. Mrs. Rix gulps for air and I realize, if we're watching this on TV now, then it's already happened minutes ago.

I run for the door, down the hallway, down the stairs. Lox and Tellie and Dekker are running behind me. The closer we get to the living room on the first floor, the louder the commotion is. I hear Dad bark out orders to someone. "Get Rix to safety!"

But it's too late.

I come to a halt when I see *him*.

Standing there, in the middle of Dekker's living room, is Ratch. LT is between him and Mr. Rix while Dad fights off a bot twice his size. Po is in the other room, fighting off more bots. A vase goes flying through the air and smashes against the wall.

"Stand down, LT," Ratch says.

"Request denied," LT says.

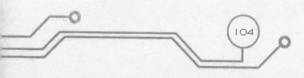

I have no idea how LT got here before us, since he didn't come down the stairs, but with LT, anything is possible. I'm just glad he's here. I have a feeling no one understands Ratch quite like LT does.

"You're wasting your time." Ratch paces to the left and LT echoes his movements. "I'm going to get him one way or the other."

"Not without going through me."

"I'll win."

"Overinflated confidence."

"This house is full of Rix's vulnerabilities."

Mr. Rix glances at Tellie and his eyes get watery.

I push Tellie back. Lox comes forward and stands tall with me. No one is getting to Tellie.

Dad kicks the bot he's fighting with his booted foot. The bot slams to the floor. Dad grabs a nearby lamp, smashes it in two over his knee, and uses the base as a stake, taking out the bot's operating system with one jab to the chest.

Now Ratch is sandwiched between Dad and LT.

"Don't provoke me, Rix," Ratch says. "Surrender and your loved ones will leave here untouched."

"Please." Mr. Rix takes a step, but LT won't let him go farther than that. "I don't want anyone to get hurt."

"He is bluffing," LT says as a red light blinks in the

back of his neck. "We outnumber him. His exit from this house is questionable, let alone with a hostage."

No one moves.

The fighting in the other room grows quiet, and Po appears in the doorway. Now Ratch is the only one left.

"I don't need to leave with a hostage." Ratch's fingers tense. "I just need to leave with Rix." His arms swing back, his feet dig into the floor, and I can tell a second too late what he's about to do.

"Tellie!" I shout when Ratch explodes into a sprint, leaps over the couch, and tosses me aside with one swoop of his arm. I fly into a bookcase, old hardcover books knocking me in the head. My ears ring. I blink back the pain, and the fuzzy halo in my vision, just in time to see Ratch wrap his claw-like fingers around Tellie's neck. He hoists her up off the floor and she gasps for air.

"No!" Mr. and Mrs. Rix say at the same time.

LT is there a second later, inches from Ratch's face. "Let her go."

"Give me Rix."

"Do not do this, friend."

Ratch sneers. His band of orange eyes glows brighter. "We are no longer friends. We are enemies. You made that choice."

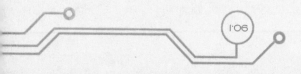

"She is just a child," LT tries.

Ratch says nothing.

Tellie scrabbles at Ratch's hand as she makes a gurgling noise in the back of her throat.

"Come on! Please!" I shout as I climb to my feet. "Someone do something!"

My insides feel like they're made of gelatin.

"I surrender," Mr. Rix says.

"Nathaniel." His wife steps forward.

"Let go of my daughter, please." Mr. Rix holds out his hands. "Please. I'll do whatever you ask."

Ratch sets Tellie to the floor again, but doesn't let her go. I breathe a little easier.

Mr. Rix makes his way to Ratch's side. "Just . . . let me say good-bye?" He slides one hand into his pants pocket, like he's trying to look casual, but deep down inside I know he's gearing out.

"You have one minute," Ratch says as he removes his hand from Tellie's throat. She gulps down air and lunges at her Dad. Mr. Rix gives her a big hug, putting one hand to the back of her neck. Tellie tenses. I worry something is wrong, but the look on her face is only confusion, not fear, so I don't say anything.

When Mr. Rix pulls away, his eyes are wet. He kisses Tellie's forehead and says, "Stay with Mr. St. Kroix. All

right? You and your mother both. You'll be safe there. Promise me that?"

"Dad," Tellie starts, but he cuts her off.

"Promise me."

She swipes at the tears streaming down her face. "I promise."

"You can trust Mr. St. Kroix," her dad says. "You can tell him anything."

Ratch grabs Mr. Rix by the arm and hauls him back. "Enough." He looks around the room before landing, finally, on LT. "If you change your mind, let me know."

The gears in his torso wind up. Click. Click. Click. He tightens an arm around Mr. Rix's torso and jets out of the house, rattling the picture frames hanging on the wall.

When he's gone, Tellie collapses to the floor, sobbing.

And all I can do is hug her, and try to make her feel safe, even though I know her life will never be the same again.

If there's one thing I understand, it's fearing Ratch.

Now he's in both our nightmares.

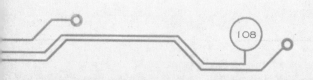

TWELVE

TELLIE DOESN'T SAY anything to anyone for a whole day. She doesn't even crack a smile when I call Lox on my Link and he performs a dance to one of Tanner Waylon's pop songs for her. She just sits in my room in the window seat staring out through the glass at the street below and the city beyond. I don't know what to say to her.

I bring her food at every meal, but she doesn't touch it.

It's been over twenty-seven hours since Ratch took her dad, so I have to get her to eat something, but the task is more difficult than math homework. And I'm not very good at math.

"If you don't eat this bowl of soup," I say, sitting next to her on the bench, "then I will have Scissor come in here and sing oldies music until you do eat. And trust me, you don't want to have to listen to Scissor sing. It's like the sound of a hundred seagulls cawing."

Tellie looks at me. The skin beneath her eyes is even darker than it was yesterday and her eyes are the color of watermelon guts.

I want to make her feel better. I want to help save her dad. I want to do something. I just need a plan first, and I'm fresh out of plans.

"Eat, please," I say. She takes the bowl from me, then a spoon. "Merril, the head bot cook, made this special for you."

She frowns. "Really?"

I nod. "You bet." I don't bother telling her that every meal Merril makes is special. "It's good too," I add. "I had some just a little while ago. It's cream of potato."

"I like potatoes," she replies as she pulls the spoon through the soup. "Got any crackers?"

"I sure do." I pull a sealed package from my pants pocket. "Ta-da."

A ghost of a smile tugs at the corners of Tellie's mouth. "Thanks, Goldfish."

"You're welcome."

She crushes a cracker and sprinkles it in the soup. We don't say anything while she eats. Surprisingly, though, I don't feel any pressure to talk. There was a time, not

that long ago, when I would have been gearing out. When the silence would have killed me dead.

But now, Tellie and I are friends, and friends don't always need to talk to enjoy each other's company. I think I read that once. Maybe in a magazine.

Tellie eats half the bowl of soup before setting it down. I hand her a bottle of water. She takes a drink, screws the cap back on one slow turn at a time.

Finally, she looks up at me and says quietly, "I have to tell you something."

I frown. "Okay."

"But you have to promise not to tell your dad."

I don't even hesitate before answering. "I promise."

She wrings her fingers together. "Double promise."

"I double promise."

She pulls a crumpled piece of paper from her pocket and hands it to me. "Yesterday, when my dad hugged me good-bye, he put this in the hood of my sweater."

I smooth out the piece of paper. There are several numbers scrawled across it, in two lines. "What does it mean?"

"They're coordinates to a location outside of Yazoo City, in what used to be Mississippi."

"Did you look it up on the satellites?"

"Yup. It's a house. Nothing else around it for miles."

"Whose house?"

"I have no idea."

"We should tell my dad. He can help."

"No!" Tellie's eyebrows sink into a V-shape. "And you promised me you wouldn't say anything."

"Why wouldn't you tell him? Whatever's at that house must be important."

Tellie leans back against the wall and pulls her knees up to her chest. "Don't you get it, Trout? Your dad is the whole reason my dad is in this mess."

I snort. "How do you figure?"

"Ratch asked him to stand down, to give the Meta-Rise to your robot friend, and your dad wouldn't do it. So now Ratch is going after important people from the UD and my dad just happens to be one of them."

I shake my head. "I don't think this has anything to do with the Meta-Rise." I think about telling her about the list of people who my dad mentioned were attached to the facility in ONY, but I'm not a hundred percent sure what it all means, and I don't want to get her hopes up. If that is why Ratch wanted Mr. Rix, then maybe he's still alive somewhere. Maybe Ratch won't hurt him.

"Whatever is at that house," Tellie says, tapping the

piece of paper still in my hands, "*is* important. And I'm going to find out what."

"You can't go there alone."

"I don't need anyone's help."

"My dad is the leader of the Meta-Rise! He should know about this. It could help save your dad."

Tellie shakes her head. "There was a reason my dad gave it to me."

"Because you were the only one he could get close to while Ratch was looking."

"Or maybe it was because he didn't trust your dad. I'm not telling him, and you swore to secrecy."

I look away and scrub my face with my hands. I *did* promise not to tell anyone, but that was before I knew what the secret was.

"Fine," I say. "I'll keep my promise, but you have to make *me* a promise. Promise me you won't do anything stupid until I can find out more. I think we need to know why Ratch wanted your dad in the first place."

I have a theory, but I need more information, and I know where to get it.

"Promise me?" I say again.

Tellie sighs. "Hurry up. My dad has already been gone an entire day." She looks out the window again.

"There's no telling what Ratch has done to him in that time."

One thing my brother is good at is keeping secrets, and my dad knows that. After all, Po kept the biggest secret from me—that our dad was alive and living in Bot Territory—for several years. If Dad trusts anyone with information about what's going on, it's Po.

I find Po in his bedroom. He's sitting on his bed, oiling his prosthetic leg. He could use an upgrade too. Dad went to get his arm upgrade this morning. After what happened with Ratch yesterday, I think everyone is thinking about upgrading. Too bad I don't have anything to upgrade.

"Hey," I say.

Po looks up. "Hey."

"So, this thing with Ratch, that's pretty cracked."

Po narrows his eyes. "You come in here to pump me for information? Because I'm not giving it to you."

Jam, he's quick. I don't know how he does it, but he always seems to know exactly what I'm thinking. It was always hard to lie to him back when we lived in Brack, when it was just us.

I sit on the edge of the bed and try to look innocent.

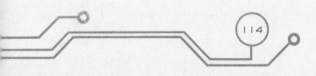

"I'm just here to have a normal conversation with my big brother."

He snorts. "Like that ever happens."

I'm losing him before I even try. "Tellie is totally gearing out about her dad. You know why Ratch wanted him, don't you?"

Po doesn't say anything, so I push on, knowing his one weakness.

"You didn't tell me Dad was alive, and look what happened. If I'd known, maybe that whole thing would have happened differently. Maybe instead of you being taken hostage, we could have broken out of the UD together. We can help Tellie."

Po sets his leg into the brackets and twists, clicking it into place. He looks over at me.

"Please?" I say, giving him my best sad, pleading, little-brother face.

That gets him. His expression softens and he cocks his head to the side. "If I tell you anything, you have to swear that it stays here, in this room. You can't tell anyone. Not Vee. Not Lox. Not Tellie. At least not yet."

I cross my fingers behind my back. "I swear."

Po cleans the seam between his real and prosthetic

leg with a special cloth. "There's a place in ONY, a facility, left over from before the war. Only four people can access it. Each has a piece of the code needed to open it. Dad says an optical scan is also required. The president is one of the four. Rix was second. And there was a third one, a woman—"

"From Fourth District," I say. "Heather Evans. The one who was kidnapped last week."

Po nods. "Yeah. And then, the fourth, a woman, an ex-congresswoman named Georgette. No one knows where she's at, since she left her job years ago and completely disappeared. Dad's looking into her location now."

I turn away, afraid that if Po looks at me, he'll know that I know more than I'm saying. Tellie has the coordinates to Georgette's location. That's what Mr. Rix gave her.

I want to tell Po the news, but I swore to Tellie that I wouldn't.

"What's inside the facility?" I ask.

Po shrugs. "No idea. And if Dad knows, he isn't telling me."

"Do the ThinkChips bought on the black market have anything to do with this?"

Po whips his head toward me. "How do you know about the ThinkChips?"

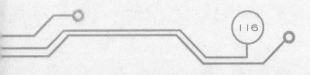

"Ummm . . ." I forgot I wasn't supposed to have that information.

"Never mind." Po shakes his head. "Maybe I don't want to know. Anyway, Dad confirmed that Ratch wasn't the one who bought the chips, but that doesn't mean he isn't connected to it."

Voices carry down the hallway. It's Vee and Marsi.

"If I find out anything more, I'll tell you," Po finishes in a rush, "but don't pester me about it. Got it?"

"I won't."

Marsi comes into the room first, with Vee trailing behind her. Marsi grins at Po. "Hey you." She goes over to him and kisses him on the lips.

"Ugggghhhh." I turn away and come face-to-face with Vee. We haven't talked since our fight. And I guess I don't blame her. I *did* cross the line. I know I hurt her feelings.

"Hey," she says quietly.

"Hey."

"Marsi," Vee says over my shoulder, "I'll catch up with you later."

"Okay." Marsi waves good-bye.

I start to say bye too, but Vee is already gone.

Later, when I'm searching the Fort for Tellie, I end up

finding her mom instead. She's in the kitchen, trying to make a cup of tea while barking orders through her Link.

"I want to pull every single source and contact I've ever had," she says, and before the person on the other end can reply, she adds, "And I want it done an hour ago. If my husband is out there somewhere, someone must have seen him. The closer we can pinpoint his location, the sooner the UD can send in troops."

She finally pauses, letting the person on the call speak, but all he gets out is: "Yes, Mrs. Rix. I'm on top of it."

"Good," Mrs. Rix says, and slams a finger into the Link screen, ending the call without a good-bye.

Merril comes up behind her and points at the tea. "Can I help with that?"

Mrs. Rix nearly jumps out of her skin. "Mother of God," she says. "Do not sneak up on me like that."

"Sorry." Merril says with a shrug.

If you aren't used to robots, Merril is an intimidating one to meet. He's big, like a rhino, with a head and chest to match. The only thing he's missing is the horn. Merril is one of the nicest robots I've ever met, though. I just think Mrs. Rix has a hard time being nice to people. Or robots.

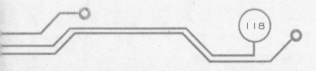

"But . . . the tea," he goes on, hardly missing a beat. "I make this delicious blend. It has this sweet, fruity taste of blueberries and strawberries, with a rich earthly undertone." He claps his hands together. "Extra-special, that blend. Extra-special. I can make you some, if you want."

"No thank you." Mrs. Rix lifts up her steaming mug. "My Earl Grey will do fine." She edges away and nearly runs into me.

"Sorry," I say real quick.

"This place is far too crowded for me," she mutters.

"Uhh . . . yeah. It's a busy place."

"I'll say."

"Have you seen Tellie?" I ask.

"Not in a few hours. She's avoiding me." She presses her lips together and exhales through her nose. "It's as if she blames me for what happened to her father. As if I had anything to do with his kidnapping. I'm doing everything in my power to bring him back."

"I know you are. She probably knows too."

"No she doesn't."

"Mrs. Rix!" Merril says. "I found that special blend! I can make you a sample!"

"Gotta go," she says to me. To Merril she says, "Perhaps later. I have a lot of work to get done." With that, she walks away, her heels punctuating her retreat.

"Did I frighten her?" Merril says. He sets the canister of tea on the counter. "I tend to do that, I think. Over-zealous, I am. That's what LT tells me. Like a Labrador retriever, he says."

"Trust me, Merril. It's not you, it's her."

He goes back to his business in the kitchen, mutter-ing something about how he needs to watch the tone of his enthusiasm.

I leave, and head off in search of Tellie. I need to tell her what I found out, in the hopes that it'll sway her not to run off on her own.

THIRTEEN

AN HOUR LATER, I've searched every corner and crevice of the Fort and still haven't found Tellie. I ask the house's system to search for her, and it comes back with a report that she isn't in the house and hasn't been in the house for more than an hour. Since she's not a registered resident, the house didn't keep as close tabs on her as it would have on, say, me, so I go to the next best source of information.

I hit up Cole.

When I first met Cole, he freaked me out. His arms are big and muscular, almost as big as my head, and tattoos cover the majority of his visible skin. Neon implants glow from the bridge of his nose, giving his eyes this menacing glint.

Turns out, Cole is just as nice as everyone else in Line Zero, so now I don't feel so weird asking him for help.

I find him in command center, which is thankfully quiet and, most importantly, absent of my dad. He'd ask what I was doing here, and then probably kick me out.

"What can I do for you, Trout?" Cole asks as he swivels around in his desk chair. He crosses his arms over his chest, which makes his biceps look really, *really* big.

"Umm . . . I need you to look something up on the house's security system."

He frowns. "Well, I need more than that. I'm not a mind reader."

I glance over my shoulder to see if anyone is listening. No one is there. "It's my friend Tellie. I can't find her in the house, and I think she left a while ago, but I need to know when she left, and which way she was going. She doesn't know Line Zero that well, so I just . . . I want to find her."

Cole wiggles his fingers. "All right then. Let's get to work." He taps several commands into his computer, then selects the day's vid footage. He finds which one he's looking for and the vid opens on the screen. "This is from two hours ago. Good place to start, just in case."

I watch over his shoulder as he fast-forwards through the recorded footage. I see people come and go from the Fort, and then finally spot Tellie.

"Stop. Right there," I say.

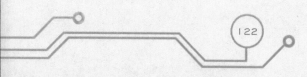

Cole rewinds the footage, then presses PLAY. Tellie leaves out the front door of the Fort and turns left, away from the town center. Worse yet, she's got her bag slung over her shoulder, and she's wearing big sunglasses and a baseball cap.

She's in disguise, and carrying all of her belongings. That's not a good sign.

"Jam," I say.

"What?" Cole asks. "Your friend isn't in trouble, is she?"

I swallow hard against the ball of dread forming in my throat. "No. She's probably just headed to the Laundromat. I forgot to tell her there was a washer and dryer in the basement." I smile, so Cole doesn't read my lies. "Thanks for your help. I'll let you get back to work now."

"No problem." He swivels back around as I dart for the elevator.

Even though Vee hasn't talked to me in days, she's the only one I can go to. She and her dad live in an apartment in Tyson's Square about two miles from the Fort. I grab one of the hoverboards from the storage room and hit the rails.

Since it's still the weekend, the hoverboard lanes are

packed with kids getting in a few more rides before school starts back up tomorrow. It takes me twice as long as usual to reach Vee's house.

I ring the doorbell and Vee's face appears on the little screen embedded in the wall. "What do you want?"

"I need your help."

"Good-bye, Trout."

"Wait."

She stops.

"I'm sorry. About what I said. I'm sorry about everything. I'm still new to all this, to robots, you know? And what Ratch did didn't help and I'm scared of him, and what he'll do, and who he might get on his side."

I take in a breath and wait.

She purses her lips and stares at me. For a second, I think I'm toast, but then Vee hits the buzzer and the door unlocks. "Come up," she says, and the screen goes blank.

I've only been to Vee's house a few times, and it seems like every time I visit, it's different. Last time I was here, the walls in the living room were white, but now the one behind the couch is purple. Paper airplanes hang from the ceiling. There's a painted portrait of a dog on the foyer wall.

Vee once told me she wants to be a designer when

she grows up. Well, a designer and a member of the Meta-Rise. I think she'd make a good one of both.

"So what's this about?" Vee says as she plops onto the sofa.

I pace the small living room and blurt out the details. "I think Tellie left to rescue her dad and I need your help finding her."

Vee sits forward, and the dangly feather earring hanging from her left ear swings forward. Her hair is twisted up tight into a bun, so the feathers stand out.

"How do you suppose I do that?"

"I know she went to Yazoo City. Do you know anything about it? About the area?"

"Not many people live there. Town is small."

"So I might have an easy time finding her, if I can get there."

Vee shrugs. "I guess so."

"Can you plot me a route?"

She shakes her head. "No way, FishKid."

At least she called me FishKid, instead of Trout, which is a good thing.

"Listen." I sit on the other end of the sofa, but keep my distance, hoping she won't throw me out the door. "Remember when Po was stuck in the UD? And our dads were going to risk their lives to rescue him? So we decided we'd do it? Remember how totally cracked that idea was?"

Vee crosses her arms in front of her. "Of course I remember, gearhead."

"Well, this is the same thing. Tellie feels like she has to do this. And she's got it far worse than we did. Our dads were home safe when we left, but Ratch *has* her dad. There's no telling what he'll do to him."

Hearing that, Vee's shoulders sink a notch. And since I think I'm winning her over, I surge on. "Tellie feels like she needs to do something important, to make her life mean something. I mean, I can understand where she's coming from and maybe you can too, and . . ."

"Stop." Vee closes her eyes and inhales. "Fine. I'll help you, but only because you're my friend and I would hate to see you take a wrong turn somewhere and end up in the Gulf of Mexico getting eaten by a shark."

She called me her friend again. Inside, I'm smiling like a goon; but outside, I'm trying to play it cool. "Like I wouldn't notice I was in the ocean?"

Vee laughs. "Sometimes, FishKid, I wonder how you've managed to make it this far without getting eaten by sharks. You're like the most innocent daredevil I've ever met."

"I don't know what that means. But it's not true."

"Whatever you say, FishKid."

I'm about to start arguing with her when she interrupts me and says, "I'll have a route planned for you by tonight. Meet me in your room at nine p.m."

"Thank you, Vee. You have no idea how much this means to me."

She smirks. "Actually, I think I do, which is *why* I'm doing it. Now go. Let me get to work!"

I hurry for the door, waving as I leave.

FOURTEEN

I WALK AROUND TOWN, hoping to waste some time before 9:00 p.m. I'm restless, knowing that Tellie is out there somewhere by herself. I know she's strong, and she's smart, but it makes me worry.

Knowing I should pack for any kind of emergency, I take my new Net tag to the main shopping center in town. Dad helped me apply for a new tag in Line Zero, one that said I was a Bot Territory citizen. He also uploaded a bunch of creds on it for me, so I could get ice cream or soda or anything I wanted whenever I wanted.

Now seems as good a time as any.

I stock up on snacks, grab an extra disposable Link, and a pair of goggles in case I need to ride a hoverboard. There are goggles at the Fort, but none like the Fairenhorts. They fit better on my face, so I'm not constantly pushing them back up, and the lenses darken in the sunlight, so I don't have to worry about fitting sunglasses into the goggles.

When I leave the grocery store, I walk around for a while longer. The sun is setting, so I know I'm getting close to 9:00. I decide to make one last stop at Scissor's.

As soon as I walk in the door, Scissor's LED panel lights up bright pink with black zebra stripes, which I think means she's proud of something she did, and also happy to see me. But I could be wrong.

"Trout! I was just thinking about you!"

"You were?"

She nods, grabs my hand, and hauls me to the back of the shop. "After I installed your dad's arm upgrade, I worked double time to get you the completed, and recently calibrated, arthropod." She holds out her arm like one of those models on a game show revealing the prize. Her audience track goes *ooohhh*.

The arthropod has gone through a mini makeover since I last saw it. It still looks like a piece of exoskeleton, like from vid games, but blue veins run beneath the steel cage. "So you never run out of boost," Scissor explains.

The claw object in the palm of the arthropod's hand is built thicker around the perimeter, the claws themselves more solid.

"It's ready for showtime!" Scissor announces, and her audience track claps in response.

"That is wrenched."

"Yaaaayyyy!" the audience says.

"So . . . I can take it now?"

"You sure can." Scissor plucks the arm from the table and hands it to me. "Did you want to wear it or do you want me to wrap it up?"

"Wrap it, please?" I don't want anyone knowing I have it yet.

"You got it."

I follow Scissor to the front of the store. It's closing time, so the sign in the front window winks off. Scissor wraps the arthropod in several layers of old packing paper and slides it into a bag.

"There you are."

I smile. "Thanks for this, Scissor. Really."

"Oh, it was my pleasure! Have fun! Don't crash into any trees!"

"Ha. Ha."

Scissor walks me out and waves good-bye.

My Link says it's just minutes after nine. Better hurry before Vee thinks I ditched her.

Vee is waiting in my room when I get back to the Fort.

"Any chance I can talk you out of this?" she asks.

I shake my head.

"Didn't think so." Vee leaves the window seat behind and comes closer, her hair turning green beneath the ceiling light. "I got your route. But the more I think about this, the more I realize how dumb the plan is."

I snort. "And breaking into a UD building with two robots to save Po wasn't?"

Vee's mouth moves as if she wants to say something back but can't think of *what* to say. She tosses me the disposable Link and I snatch it from the air.

"There's your route," she says. "Don't get your head fried off by a rogue bot. Or something worse."

"What's worse than that?"

"I'm sure there are lots of things. Ax murders. Man-eating snakes. Toxic mold. I could go on."

"No. Don't." My lungs tighten with fear. Maybe this is a bad idea. Well, I *know* it's a bad idea, but I don't see any other choice. I could tell Dad, but what if he

decided not to go after Tellie? She is the daughter of one of his enemies. He doesn't owe her anything. Or what if he takes too long putting together a search team and Tellie is hurt in the meantime?

I don't want to risk it. It's better if I go now. Maybe I can find her and bring her home before anyone knows we're gone.

"Thanks again, Vee," I say quietly.

She waves at me, as if she can't handle a lot of sentimental nonsense at one time. I admire her for that. I wish I could be as tough as her.

"You want to come with me?" I don't look at her when I ask. I don't want her to know that I don't want to go alone. That I'm scared.

"I can't, FishKid," she answers. "Not this time."

I shrug. "It's no big deal."

We stand there for what seems like a long time before one of us speaks. Vee is the first one to break the silence. "When are you leaving?"

"After dark, probably. When everyone is in bed."

She nods, like that makes sense. "How are you traveling?"

"Err . . . I haven't figured that out yet. Hoverboard, probably."

"That'll take you too long." She thinks for a second,

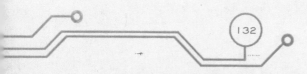

tapping her mouth with her fingers. "I might have a better idea. I'll message you in a bit to let you know if it works out."

"Okay. Sounds good. I guess I'll just—"

She lunges at me, cutting me off, and wraps her arms around me in a hug. Her feather earring tickles my neck. "Don't get hurt, okay? Promise me."

"I promise."

"Call my Link if you need me. I don't care what time it is."

"Okay."

"And FishKid?"

"Yeah?"

"You smell like dirty feet."

I laugh. Vee does too.

When she pulls away, she messes up my hair, even though she knows that drives me nuclear. I don't mind, though. At least not this time.

We say our good-byes. I watch her leave, and when I hear the click of the door, my heart sinks.

FIFTEEN

AT 11:50 P.M., I creep out of my room. I got a message on my Link from Vee an hour ago that said to go to Yan's parents' shop on the east side of town at 12:15 a.m. I didn't ask questions, and said I'd be there.

The hall outside my room is silent, and dark save for a flash of moonlight stealing through the windows. I tiptoe toward Po's room. A part of me secretly hopes he's awake and asks why I'm creeping around the Fort at midnight.

But when I push in his door, I find him sprawled on his stomach on the bed, his arms folded beneath his pillow. A loud, snarly snore rumbles out of him. Po hasn't slept well enough to snore in a long time.

His fake leg is lying on the floor next to the bedside table.

If I'm going to run away to a place I've never been, to a place that might not even be safe, I want to leave someone a note to let them know where I'm going. I could leave Po a note on his bedside table, or his dresser, but who knows when he'd find it. *If* he'd find it.

There's one way I know he'll get the message.

I snatch his fake leg and scurry out of the room and back to my room. I set his leg on the foot of my bed and tape a piece of paper to its knee.

Po,

Tellie's dad gave her coordinates to a place in Yazoo City right before Ratch took him. She left today without telling anyone. She thinks the coordinates will lead her to saving her dad, but I think they go to Georgette's house.

Ask Vee for a map. Sorry I left without telling you, but Tellie made me swear to keep her secret. She's scared, Po. I guess we all are.

Tell Dad not to be mad.

Trout

With my backup plan in place, I scoop up my bag, snatch a hoverboard, and sneak out of the Fort.

Yan's family's shop is only a ten-minute board ride away from the Fort, so I arrive before 12:15 a.m. and have to wait.

Vee's instructions said to wait in the back, so I find a bench pushed up against the brick wall and plop down, feeling restless, but curious, and hoping I don't have to wait too long.

A car pulls into the empty lot at exactly 12:15. At first I think it's someone who's tracked me, maybe Dad, or LT, or even Po. But when the car pulls up next to me, I realize it can't be any of them. This car is too fancy to belong to anyone from the Fort.

The door pops open and Yan pokes his head out, his neon tooth implants glowing in the darkness.

"Hey Trout!" he says.

"Yan? What are you doing here?"

He steps out onto the pavement, his shoes crunching over loose pebbles. "Vee told me about your situation and said you needed to borrow a car."

I eye the car again. A silver emblem on the hood reads *Rhy-T*. It's a model made by one of the most expensive car manufactures in the world. It's a self-driving car, that

much I know. And I think it's supposed to have a mini kitchen in the back, along with a full entertainment center, complete with a vid counsel, and thousands of pre-loaded movies.

It's probably more expensive than my life is worth.

"I can't take that," I say, and wave my hands back and forth just in case Yan didn't hear me. "What if something happens to it?"

It's not like I'm taking a casual ride through the countryside, after all. With my luck, it'll get crushed beneath the foot of a giant bot.

"It's got insurance, you goon." Yan comes over to my side and puts his arm around my shoulders. "Plus, not to sound like a spoiled rat head, but this isn't my only car. I've got another at home. A newer one, anyway."

I stammer something about it not being right, but Yan stops me.

"Trout, listen buddy." He withdraws his arm and stands in front of me. "Vee told me you've got something super-important to do. And if I know you, and I know your fam, important is important. Everyone in school knows you helped save Edge Flats when the UD attacked. If Trout needs a car for one of his save-the-world missions, then I'm going to provide a car.

"Get me?"

"You know about Edge Flats?"

He grins. "Course I do! The first day of school, it was all everyone talked about. About how kila you were."

Suddenly I realize maybe I'm not as lame as I thought I was. Maybe I'm not as invisible as I thought I was.

I look past Yan at the Rhy-T again. I do want to accept his gift. It'll get me there in a third of the time a hoverboard would. Plus, I'd be a lot safer in a car, with doors that locked. There's no telling what I might run into on the journey.

"Are you sure you don't mind?"

He gives a quick nod of his head. "Absolutely."

"All right." I hold out my hand, and we shake. "Thanks, Yan."

"You're welcome, my friend."

I climb in the car and Yan gives me a quick run-down of the controls. After he says good-bye and shuts the door behind him, I punch in my first nav point and the car silently glides out of the parking lot.

It's surprisingly easy to escape Line Zero this time. Easier than it was when I was with Vee trying to break into Texas. I suppose no one really cares if you move farther into Bot Territory.

A half hour after leaving my room, Line Zero is nothing but a few streetlights behind me, dotting the

darkness in my rearview mirror. I settle into the leather bucket seat and read a comic book on the car's dash SimPad, then play with a hybrid animal app, then read another comic book.

An hour later, I check the route on the disposable Link Vee gave me and type in the next nav point on the car's system. According to the map, I'm just outside of a town that used to be Tallulah. Rain splatters on the windshield. The wind picks up, pushing the car back and forth on the road. The trees bend, branches swaying in the wind. It's eerie, and I've never wanted to go home more than I do now.

For the next half hour, I keep careful watch on the map, and my surroundings, hoping that by some miracle I'll spot Tellie. I'm close enough to Line Zero that getting home before the Fort wakes up seems possible.

The car comes around a bend in the road where distant city lights dot the horizon.

"Approximately seven miles to Tallulah," the car says.

The car rounds one final curve and the lights are no longer pinpricks in the dark, but shinning pools of light on the grimy, oily pavement.

I had been picturing a smaller version of Line Zero, but Tallulah is nothing like that. As the car slows, and creeps into town, I realize this city matches the image I had of Bot Territory before I left the UD.

An industrial wasteland.

The road narrows. The car slows even more. I roll down the window and catch the smell of melted rubber and burning wires. There are no people on the streets, no other cars. The hover rails here are barely working, winking on and off in some sections. I spot a pile of empty robot shells on one street corner, and several old gears on another.

There is no movement, anywhere.

I've almost given up hope on finding Tellie here, until I see a car pulled over on the side of the road, one block up, its undercarriage hoverpoints still glowing faintly in the dark.

"Stop," I tell the car, and it pulls over, right behind the abandoned car. I get out. The air is warm and sticky with humidity, and it clings to my skin like a wet bedsheet. I'm suddenly doubting the clothes I wore—a pair of pants tucked into combat boots and a T-shirt. Maybe I should have worn shorts. Then again, shorts aren't exactly the kind of clothes you wear when you're on a top-gear mission.

I scan the street. "Tellie?" I call, keeping my voice

low, as if talking too loud will wake the scary monsters or something.

I grunt, and shake my head. "You're being ridiculous, Trout."

Movement catches my eye. I freeze.

A bot with eight spindly legs and a body low to the ground, like a giant spider, crawls over the roof of a one-story building and stops at the corner to watch me. Every nerve, joint, and muscle in my body turns to stone.

I've never seen anything like it.

This isn't good. Not good at all.

The spider takes a few more creepy-crawly steps and I bolt down the sidewalk, cross the street, and then run another two blocks before stopping. I lean into the building behind me to catch my breath. I guess I need to exercise more, because I'm dead already and I haven't run that far.

The building is cold through my T-shirt, like metal that sat out in the dark too long. Hands on my knees, hunched over, I pull in several deep breaths. Sweat beads on my forehead.

I'm about to push away from the wall and start walking again, when the building moves behind me.

Moves. Like a living thing.

I leap away and gape at what I thought was a building, but is very clearly *not,* as it shudders and groans and straightens out, standing on two feet.

It's a massive robot, as tall as a giraffe, with shoulders as wide as an elephant. A gear clicks, something whirs, and its head swivels toward me, several lights in its face blinking on. I squint, bringing my arm up to shield my eyes as a spotlight winks on, blinding me.

I know what that is. I've read about them in war books, seen them on TV. I even have a vid game about them.

It's an old war bot. One of the exoskeleton frontline bots. They were used on the front lines because they were massive and intimidating. And they were given simple programming. Their orders were usually *Shoot anything human.*

I am so notched.

"Trout!" someone screams, and it takes me a second to realize it's Tellie.

She races toward me, grabs my hand, and yanks me in the opposite direction as the war bot takes one lumbering footstep in our direction. The ground shakes beneath us, the vibration shooting up my legs.

"Tellie," I say, breathless. "You're okay . . ."

She yells something to me, but I can't hear her over the thundering of the bot's footsteps and the thumping of my heart. "What did you say?" I ask.

We whip around a street corner and come to a sliding halt.

I see the orange glow first, reflecting off cracked windows and oily streets. Then the silhouette of a robot, a human-sized robot, whose body is made of flat black composite.

"I said," Tellie replies, "Ratch is here."

SIXTEEN

MY GUTS SINK to my feet. If I thought the exoskeleton war bot was scary, the bot I see in front of me is darn near terrifying.

"Trout," he says. "Nice to see you."

Tellie grits her teeth. "We want my dad back!"

Ratch spreads out his arms. "He isn't here. Clearly." He turns back to me. "Where are you going, Trout? Maybe we can travel together."

"I'm never going anywhere with you ever again. No one trusts you anymore, Ratch. Not even LT."

Ratch pauses. I realize in an instant that I've hit a soft spot. LT. If Ratch had a weakness, I think LT would be it. They're like brothers. Or at least they were once.

Ratch takes a few more steps, and Tellie and I mirror him, stepping backward. "You know nothing about this, or about me, or LT," he says. "Don't use a gun until you're sure you've loaded the proper ammunition."

I swallow hard against the tightness in my throat

and narrow my eyes. "I know you turned on LT. Your own kind. I thought that's what you were standing up for. For robots. Apparently you don't care about them either."

"I turned on *you*," Ratch answers. "LT could get out of that mess if he truly wanted to."

I knew Ratch disliked humans, but I didn't know his hatred was aimed at me.

"I've never done anything to you."

"You ended up saving Edge Flats, didn't you? A twelve-year-old boy saved an entire city. Tell me that's not something to be wary of. I've seen your potential since the moment I met you, Trout." He tilts his head down, leveling me with his gaze. "If only you could see it too. You'd bring down nations."

Tellie threads her fingers with mine, reminding me that she's here, that we're still in danger. For a second, what Ratch said, and the way he said it, made me feel like maybe we weren't enemies after all.

But we are. That will never change.

If only LT were here to help me. I don't know how to defeat Ratch. He's too smart, too clever. He uses words as weapons just as much as a gun.

What was I thinking coming out here by myself? What was Tellie thinking?

"So," Ratch goes on, "where did you say you were going? Was it Yazoo City?"

"No," I answer.

"Lie," Ratch counters.

The exoskeleton bot turns the corner toward us, his lumbering footsteps jarring our bones. The guns on his forearms start turning, letting out a high-pitched whine as the barrels light up red.

"Run," I shout, and Tellie takes off at a sprint with me tailing right behind her.

We only make it ten steps before Ratch is in front of us, cutting us off with his warp speed.

The exo-bot presses closer.

We're trapped.

I scan the street, looking for an alternate exit, or at the very least a weapon. Instead, I see dozens and dozens of eyes staring back at us over the roofs of the abandon buildings.

Spider bots.

Hundreds of 'em. Their legs click across the roof tiles as they settle into place.

Running is useless. There's no way to escape.

I glance over my shoulder at the exo-bot, who's standing right over the top of a manhole cover in the middle of the street.

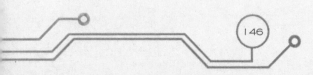

A plan starts to form in my head.

I hold up my hands. "What is it you want, Ratch?" I take two steps back and gesture at Tellie, hoping she'll follow.

She does.

"Tell me where you're going. That's all I need to know. Exact coordinates."

"You already know where we're going."

"I need an address."

Tellie shakes her head. "We don't have that."

"Lie. Again." The gears in Ratch's neck swivel silently as he cocks his head in an un-humanlike way.

We take several more steps backward. I can feel the heat output of the massive exo-bot as we near him.

How many more steps? I want to look, but if I do, I'm worried Ratch will know what I'm up to.

The spiders scuttle over the rooftops as they track our movements.

"What are you doing?" Tellie whispers through gritted teeth.

"The address?" Ratch repeats.

"It's—"

"Don't say anything!" Tellie says.

"It's East End Yazoo City, a green building on Red-Tail Avenue."

Ratch tilts his head to the other side, as if he's listening carefully to the beating of my heart and the rise of my voice, trying to decide whether I'm lying.

I am. I don't know if there's even a RedTail Avenue in Yazoo City. I just blurted the first name that came to mind.

"Seize them," he says.

The exo-bot takes a thundering step. Hundreds of spiders come pouring over the buildings like water over a cliff.

"Trout!" Tellie shrieks.

The exo-bot makes a grab for us. "Duck!" I scream, and Tellie and I hit the pavement, crouching like cats. When the bot straightens, I dive between his legs, lift up on the manhole cover, and . . . it doesn't open.

The spiders close in.

Tellie slams into me.

I yank on the cover.

The exo-bot twists in an unnatural position, trying to find us beneath him, and several rusted pieces of metal break off, raining down on us. Tellie wraps her arms over the top of her head, shielding herself.

A spider bot latches on to Tellie's leg and she kicks and flails, trying to shake it loose. I bat at it as a second spider leaps off the foot of the exo-bot onto

my shoulder, its spindly legs digging into my neck.

No time to focus on the spiders. I tug at the manhole cover one more time and it budges one tiny little millimeter. I dig my feet in as another spider crawls over my back. I pull and pull and the cover pops off, finally! I push Tellie down the darkened hole. She shrieks and I scurry after her, pulling the cover in place over us.

Tellie continues to scream in the darkness. I make it down next to her and, somehow, without any light, manage to tear the spider from her hair and smash it beneath my feet. I work on the two I brought down with us, tossing one into the concrete wall, where it shatters into a million pieces.

The last one Tellie grabs from my shoulder. She hoists it over her head. As my eyes adjust to the darkness, I see the spider's legs flailing as it searches for something to grab hold of.

But Tellie brings it down, slamming it into the floor once, twice, three times, till it's nothing but bits of metal and plastic and wire.

I heave a breath.

"That was kila," Tellie says. She pushes sweaty, matted hair from her face as the manhole cover shudders above.

"Kila?" I ask.

She shrugs. "I heard someone say it in Line Zero and I decided I like it."

I shake my head. My dad used to use the word *resilient* a lot, back before the war, when he was talking about the weeds in his garden, and I think it can be used to describe Tellie right now.

She's sweaty, covered in oil from the broken spider bot, and she's talking about slang.

I just smile at her and say, "We better get moving."

We push farther into the darkness.

We don't dare turn on a light for fear Ratch will use it to spot us. We stumble ahead, holding on to each other for balance. We turn so many corners that I have no idea where we are. Not that it matters. As long as we're far from Ratch.

"Shh," Tellie says, and pulls me to a stop.

I listen. I listen so hard, my ears start to ring. "I don't hear anything."

"That's what I mean. We must have lost them."

I let out a breath of relief. "You scared me."

"Sorry."

We walk for another few minutes in silence, just in case, but then I can't stand it any longer, and besides, I have a thing or two to say to Tellie.

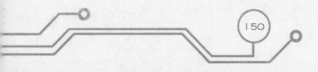

"Why did you leave without telling me?"

It's hard making out her face in the dark, but I think I see her eyes pinch at the corners, which must mean she's either annoyed that I asked, or embarrassed that she took off so suddenly without a clear plan.

"I don't know, Trout. I guess I thought this was my problem. Not yours. I didn't want to ask for your help. Or anyone else's. It's *my* dad who needs saving."

"Yeah, but don't you remember—a few months ago it was my dad who was missing. And who was the one person who helped me try to find him?"

She pauses. "That was different."

"No it wasn't. I owe you for helping me make that vid."

She surges forward. "Yeah, but what could you possibly do to help me? This isn't a problem that can be solved with a vid! I just need to get to the coordinates my dad sent me to—"

"I know where they lead," I blurt.

She stops again. "You do? Where?"

"They go to a woman's house. Georgette. She used to be a congresswoman."

"How do you know that?"

"Because I asked Po. Just like I told you I was going to. He told me why Ratch wanted your dad." I fill her

in on all the details I know, about the secret facility in ONY, the four people who have pieces of the code to enter it.

"Georgette is the last one," I continue. "That's why Ratch wanted to know where we were going. He's looking for Georgette too."

"Then we need to get to her first." Tellie hurries forward, but I grab her by the wrist.

"We need to go back to the Fort and tell my dad. He can help Georgette. He can help save your dad too."

"We're already halfway there, Trout." She pulls away from me and throws her arms up. "If we go back now, Ratch will beat us there."

"And what are we going to do to stop him?"

"If we get there first, we won't have to stop anything."

I frown. "I'm confused."

"If we find Georgette first, she can tell us where the facility is, and if we find the facility, we can save my dad."

She sets her hands on her hips and stands tall. For a second I see the old Tellie, the one who yelled at me in the concession center in the park in Brack. The same Tellie who hardly ever talked to me, who barely knew I existed. The same Tellie who had a mom and a dad and

a big fancy house and everything anyone could ever want.

Seeing that old Tellie makes me realize, all of a sudden, how different this new Tellie is. She's stronger, more understanding, nicer too, or at least to me. But the new Tellie no longer has that nice house, at least not while Ratch is out there, and this new Tellie's dad is in trouble.

The old Tellie never would have risked her life to go on this cracked mission, but new Tellie would, and new Trout wants to help her.

"All right," I say. "Then we'll go to Georgette's."

"We?" she echoes.

"I'm coming with you. Obviously."

The corners of her mouth quirk up in a smile. "Thanks, Goldfish."

I shrug. "It's no big deal."

"Yes it is."

We stare at each other like a couple of toads on a log for a second, before I say, "Let's get moving," and Tellie says, "Agreed." And then we move.

SEVENTEEN

WE FIND A ladder out of the tunnels an hour later.

I'm the first one up. I pop open the manhole cover with a little bit of grunting and find myself in the middle of a deserted street. There are no lights for miles, so I tap in a command on my Link and open the flashlight function.

I help Tellie aboveground and then replace the manhole cover. We look around, hands on our hips.

Several hovercars are parked at the curbs, their boost systems smashed beneath them. Their windows are either missing, or cracked, or caked with dust. An old RR5 across the street is missing all its doors. The buildings that used to make up whatever small town this was are dark, their brick exteriors pitted. I find myself thinking the broken-down bricks are good for climbing, and then tell myself real quick to stop thinking that way because someone like me used to call this place home and now look at it.

It's like everyone picked up and left at the exact same time. The place feels haunted, like it's watching me, but also like it's lonely and wants its old life back.

I take a few steps down the middle of the street. Something crunches beneath my foot. It's a plastic toy, a baby rattle, I think, with a holo projector built into the top. It probably displayed an image of the stars, or maybe the baby's mom.

"This is what I pictured Bot Territory to look like," Tellie says. "Dead. And abandoned. It's creepy."

"There are a lot of places like this, though. Remember the ghost town we learned about in school? What was it . . ."

"Vulture City," Tellie answers for me.

"Yeah. This is just another ghost town. Someday our grandkids will be learning about this place."

"Ewww."

"Why ewwww?"

"I don't even want to think about having kids, let alone grandkids!" She laughs. "Sometimes you crack me up."

"Makes you wonder why we were never friends in school, doesn't it?"

Her laughter fades away. "Yeah, I guess so. But we're friends now. That's all that matters."

We follow the main road out of town. Tellie gives me the exact coordinates to Georgette's house and I put them into my disposable Link. We only went two miles out of our way when we were in the tunnels, so, when my Link finally connects to the system, I get us back on track and headed in the right direction.

Vee was nice enough to plot us a route around Yazoo. It saves us some time, and now I think it might save our lives if Ratch is already there.

The sun starts to creep upward, turning the sky a dull shade of blue when we reach the dirt road we're supposed to turn on, where the mysterious Georgette lives.

"Is that it?" Tellie points at a large farmhouse just around the next curve in the road. There are barely any trees, just open fields of overgrown grass, so it's easy to see the house in the distance.

I check my Link, and the red dot that represents our destination blinks just ahead. "Yeah, I think that's it."

"It doesn't look like anyone lives there."

She's right. The driveway is empty. There are no lights on, but then again, it's not even 6:00 a.m. so maybe Georgette is still sleeping.

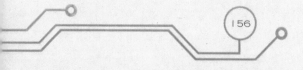

We follow the road down a hill, around a bend. We slow as we near the house. There's an old mailbox post at the end of the dirt driveway, with a mailbox hanging off the top like a cherry sliding off a melting sundae. The post says, in faded black letters, *Mulhalley*.

Now that we're closer, I give the house a good scan. The front porch wraps around the entire house, and there are pieces of white wicker furniture all over the place, in no particular order. A swing chained to the porch ceiling creaks as a gust of wind gives it a push. Flowers pour out of a pot at the top of the porch steps. There are purple flowers, and white and pink too.

And if the flowers are alive, and in good shape, that must mean someone is taking care of them.

"What do you think?" I whisper to Tellie, never taking my eyes off the house.

"I say we go up there and knock on the door."

I start to argue that maybe we should think about this first, that if Georgette has been hiding from the government for years, then the last thing she's going to do is invite in a couple of kids who are looking for her. But Tellie marches away from me, before I can object, and before I know it, she's on the front porch knocking on the door.

I make it up the three steps to the porch just as the

front door creaks open and an old woman peers out.

My heart plummets to my knees and then keeps right on going, pooling in my toes.

The woman is ancient. Or maybe it's just that she hasn't had any of the facial surgeries that all the women back in the UD have, to erase some of their wrinkles and make their skin glow golden. Po said they do that so they look twenty again, because no one wants to get old.

The skin around this woman's eyes droops like the skin on a basset hound. Her lips are dry, and her nose is peeling from an old sunburn. But when she looks at us through the screen door, she smiles and her eyes light up.

"I know you," she says, and nods at me. Then she peers at Tellie. "And I know you too."

"You do?" Tellie asks.

"Aidan St. Kroix and Tellie Rix. I'd say it's a pleasure to meet you, but if you're here, something must be wrong." Her voice is airy, but with a slight rasp, like wind whistling over a lake. She pushes the screen door all the way open and steps outside, wiping her hands on a red-and-white-checkered towel. "I haven't checked the news in a couple of days. Uses up a lot of my solar power, you see."

"We need your help," Tellie says. "My dad was kid-

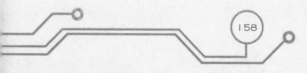

napped and he gave me your address before he was taken."

"Ahhh." She holds the door open for us. "Best get inside, then. I imagine we have a lot of talking to do."

We enter into a foyer where a big round table takes up the majority of the space. White roses are stuffed into a bubble vase in the center of the table. There's a framed picture sitting beneath the roses. On a closer look, I see it's a young woman with Georgette's kind eyes. It must be her daughter. I heard Dad talking about her last week. She's a fashion designer in 1st District.

"Come back to the kitchen," Georgette says, and skirts around the table. "I was just making some biscuits."

We follow hesitantly, passing a sitting room stuffed with red furniture, and a library with empty bookcases. Georgette hums to herself as she disappears through the third doorway on the right.

When I enter the kitchen behind Tellie, I instantly notice two things: The kitchen smells like fresh baked bread and chili, and there's a robot standing over the stovetop.

Georgette nods at the bot. "This is Linda. Why don't you say hi, Linda?"

The bot slowly swivels toward us, a wooden spoon in her left hand. Chili sauce drips off the end and splatters on the floor, but Linda doesn't notice.

"Good night!" she says in a chipper, high-pitched voice.

"She means good morning," Georgette explains. "She has a blip in her programming somewhere and I'm no techie, so I don't know how to fix her. She switches words around a lot, and says the wrong thing at the wrong time. You'll get used to it."

Tellie hovers near the doorway, eyeing the bot. Even though she's spent more than a day in Line Zero, surrounded by bots, I know she hasn't gotten used to them.

Georgette notices Tellie's apprehension. "Linda won't bite. I promise."

Tellie takes a few steps into the kitchen. "So . . . you're the last person with the code."

Georgette looks up. "The president is gone?"

Tellie and I nod.

Georgette lets out a breath and rubs her forehead as if massaging a headache that suddenly bloomed there. "That's not good." She eases into a chair at the table situated beneath a bank of windows and stares out at the field beyond.

We give her a minute to process the news.

Linda is the first to break the silence. "This chili is blazing cold. Woo. Too much chili powder."

Georgette manages a smile at Linda's word mix-up, but then she frowns when she looks at us. "Last I had heard, we were only missing Heather Evans from Fourth District." She pats the chair next to her. "Sit down. Bring me up to speed."

Tellie is the one to start, beginning with the president's kidnapping, then her dad's kidnapping the same day.

"Seems odd that Ratch would go after the president before me or Rix, though . . . now that I think about it . . . perhaps that was a good strategy. If he was the last man standing, his security detail would have been hefty." She takes a sip of the tea Linda made for her, then: "What else do you know?"

We tell her about Ratch, and the ThinkChips purchased on the black market.

"Well, that's not a good sign," she says, and gets up from the table.

"Why?" I ask.

She tastes the chili. "Oh. I like that. Spicy chili is my favorite. Good job, Linda."

"Thank you."

"Why?" Tellie repeats.

"Breakfast first." Georgette goes to the glass-fronted refrigerator and starts pulling out things.

Linda grabs a clean pan. "What would you all like? I can scramble you up some chickens."

Tellie and I look at Georgette for a translation.

"Scramble you up some eggs, she means. Naturally."

"We can't sit here and eat breakfast when Ratch is out there somewhere looking for you," Tellie says.

"Why not?" Georgette hands Linda the carton of eggs. "I'm not going to let a rogue robot ruin my breakfast. That would just be a tragedy."

Since my stomach has been growling all night, I nod quickly. "She's right, you know."

Tellie gives me a look.

"What?" I say. "I'm starving."

"Then it's settled. We'll talk more over breakfast, huh?" Georgette says. "I can't digest any more bad news until I can digest my eggs."

Linda sets to work, scrambling at least a dozen "chickens," and by the time those are done, Georgette has biscuits cooling on a rack on the table.

We all sit down in the official fancy dining room in the back of the house to eat. It's a circular room with a table in the center. Sunlight now pours through the window, turning the dust in the air a bright golden color.

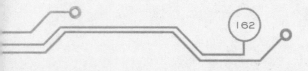

I toss some salt and pepper on my eggs, take one bite, and then stop chewing. Something, or someone, is screaming outside and I think they're screaming my name. Tellie and I glance at each other across the table. I swallow the eggs that have now turned to dust in my mouth.

Po found us. Or maybe my dad. Either way, we're screwed. And Tellie is going to be so mad at me when she finds out I left Po a note.

I set my fork down. It clinks against the edge of the plate.

"Trout!" they say again, and I realize in an instant it *is* Po, and he doesn't sound mad at all, he sounds panicked.

I shove my chair back. Tellie leaps to her feet.

"What's going on?" Georgette asks, peering out the window. "Who is that?"

"It's my brother," I say, and bolt for the front door.

I hesitate on the porch as I scan the horizon for him, unsure of what I'll find, or if I somehow read his tone of voice wrong and he really is steaming mad.

But what I see at the bend in the road is far worse than a ticked-off Po.

I see him stumbling toward us, LT at his side, and Marsi in Po's arms, hanging there like an overcooked

163

noodle. Her white shirt is stained dark red, and I know, despite the distance still between us, that it's blood.

"Po!" I start running toward him with Tellie on my heels.

I skid to a stop on the dirt road, but Po keeps on going for the house. "She's lost a lot of blood. I'm not a match for her. LT tested me. We patched her up on our way here, but we did a crappy job with what we had." He doesn't stop to wait for me. "Does Georgette have medical supplies?"

I have to run harder to keep up with him. I don't know how he's managing it with his bum leg. "I don't know. We just got here." LT zooms ahead of us to explain to Georgette who he is, and who Po and Marsi are.

"What happened?" I ask Po.

"We were attacked." He repositions Marsi in his arms. Sweat pours down his forehead. "In the middle of the night. It was an army of robots with Ratch at the forefront. They attacked the Fort first. I wanted to stay to fight, but Marsi . . ." His voice wavers.

"What about Dad?" I ask, my own voice cracking. I'm afraid of what Po's answer will be, but I have to know what it is.

"He and his team were evacuating the Fort. There's a

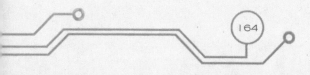

hidden emergency exit in the basement. That's how we got out. They were going to try to evacuate the rest of the city, but I don't know if they got that far."

"My mom?" Tellie asks. "What about my mom?"

"She's fine," Po says quickly. "She found a cameraman and started reporting."

That sounds like Mrs. Rix, I think. She wouldn't stop working even in the middle of the apocalypse. Not when it came to reporting a top story. I just hope she's careful for Tellie's sake.

Po hops up the two steps to the porch, gritting his teeth, a pinch of pain at the corners of his eyes. His bum leg must be killing him.

"Go on in," Linda, the bot, says when she meets us at the front door.

We find Georgette in the library. "Put her on the table here." She points to the long redwood table where a thick blanket has been spread over the top. LT blasts into the room, his arms overloaded with medical supplies.

Po gently puts Marsi on the table. Her head lolls to the side. Her eyes have been shut since I met Po on the road, and her breathing is super-shallow.

My own chest tightens, and my stomach feels all woozy, like a hundred goldfish are swimming inside.

What if Marsi dies? I don't know if my brother can handle it. I don't know if I can.

"I need scissors," Georgette says. LT hands her a pair and she splits Marsi's shirt up the middle, exposing her stomach and her blood-stained bra.

"You should go," Po says, scooting me toward the door.

"But . . ."

"Go!"

I ram into Tellie as we both try to leave the room in a hurry. Po slides the pocket doors shut behind us with a loud bang.

And Tellie and I have no choice but to sit and wait.

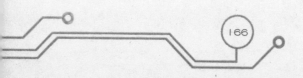

EIGHTEEN

Po COMES STUMBLING out of the room an hour later with blood all over his clothes and a dazed look in his eyes. Tellie and I leap to our feet.

"Is she okay?" I ask. "Marsi," I add, as if he had somehow forgotten who I meant. "What about the blood she lost?"

Po scrubs at his face with one hand. There's a clean shirt in his other hand. "Turns out your friend Georgette is O positive. She donated."

"Good. That's good, right?"

"Yeah. It means Marsi is stabilized. For now." He rips off his stained shirt and holds it in his hand and looks around for a place to toss it. But there isn't one, so he just balls it up and stares at it.

"I'll take care of it," Tellie offers. Po hands it to her before tugging the clean white T-shirt on. And then he just freezes in place. Not moving. Not blinking. It doesn't even seem like he's breathing.

Tellie's footsteps disappear down the hallway, so the only sound in the room is the ticking of an old clock, the ones with letters for numbers.

"Po?" I whisper.

"I'm glad you weren't there," he says, and finally breaks down.

He covers his face with his hands and his shoulders shake and soon he's sobbing. I swallow the wedge in my throat. I don't know what to do or say that will make any of this better. If I'd been there when the attack started . . . maybe I could have done something . . . maybe Marsi would be okay.

Po sucks in a long, raspy breath and wipes off his face. "Sorry. Sorry. I just . . ."

I shrug. "It's okay." I instantly regret saying it. It's lame, for one; and two, well, I've never seen my brother gear out like this, and I feel like I need something bigger to say. Something that's important.

Except I don't have anything. So I just keep my mouth shut.

"When I first read your note," Po says a minute later, "I was furious. I couldn't believe you would be so stupid. Running off in the middle of the night, you and Tellie Rix of all people. Neither of you knows anything about Bot Territory!" His voice rises in volume. "Right away

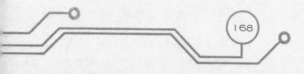

I started wondering if you were okay." He scratches at the back of his head and looks away. "When they attacked, the anger was gone"—he snaps his fingers—"like that. And I was so grateful you weren't in Line Zero. You could have—" His face scrunches up and he grits his teeth, sucking in air through his nose. "I'm just glad you're okay."

"I'm sorry." I fidget with the bottom of my shirt. "But . . . we're all okay now. Marsi is going to be okay. I know it."

Po nods his head once, but his eyes are glassy again like he's not sure if he believes me. And I guess I don't know if I should believe me either.

"How did you find us?" I ask. "Did Vee give you the map?"

"Yeah. She gave me the map on a disposable Link."

"Did she get out? Is she okay?"

"I think so. I think she was with Scissor."

"Should we go back?" I take two steps around the red couch between us. "Vee could be hurt. Or Dad could be . . ."

"No." Po shakes his head. "No way. Not till we hear from Dad first."

"But—" I start, and he cuts me off real quick.

"Dad gave me a mission, Trout. To find you and

make sure you and Marsi were safe. Second to that, LT and I were to make sure Georgette was being guarded. I've done all of those things. Now we wait. Dad will get hold of us when he can. And Marsi will be on her feet in a few days. That's when we'll leave."

I sit down on the couch and Po sits at the other end. "What happened to Marsi, anyway?" I ask.

Po's shoulders sag an inch. "She was shot in the back while we escaped."

My stomach goes all squirrely, and reminds me that one second we can be happy, and the next could be disastrous.

Maybe I did rush into this mission with Tellie. Maybe I was stupid to risk my life. An image of Ratch comes to mind, followed closely by a snapshot of the exoskeleton robot and the hundreds of spider bots that surrounded us.

Which makes me wonder . . . if Ratch was attacking us in Tallulah, then how was he also attacking in Line Zero?

"Are you sure you saw Ratch at the attack?" I ask.

"Positive. Why?"

I chew at my lower lip, thinking.

"Trout?" Po says.

"Well . . . there's something I haven't told you yet . . . about Ratch."

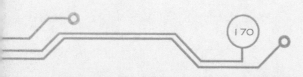

"Spit it out."

"He attacked Tellie and me in Tallulah last night."

Po narrows his eyes. "He what?"

"Which means he was in two places at the same time."

Po and I think about that for a minute, before Po says, "Someone bought ten thousand illegal ThinkChips on the black market."

"But not Ratch," I say.

"Doesn't mean he wasn't attached to the purchase."

"True."

"Dad thought the extra ThinkChips were going to an army of bots, which maybe was true, but—"

"They aren't just any bots, are they?"

All the color leaves Po's face, so he looks like a stone statue of himself as he says, "He's making clones of himself."

Po goes in search of LT, to tell him our theory, while I go in search of Georgette. I find her in the kitchen, hunched over a bowl of steaming soup. She's paler than when I last saw her, and her eyes look hollow.

"Can I talk to you about something?" I ask her.

She nods and crushes up a handful of crackers into her soup as I relay the conversation Po and I just had.

When I finish, she says, "Interesting," and that's it.

"Interesting?" I say. "It's cracked!"

"Well, I knew right away what Ratch was doing when you told me about the ThinkChips. It's why he's after the four of us with the facility codes in the first place. I just had no idea he was making clones of himself. But now that I think about it . . . it does make sense. He's the most wanted criminal on the continent. Makes it harder to catch him if you don't know which him is *him*."

"Wait." I hold out my hand. "*Why* is he after the codes? What's in the facility?"

I've wanted this answer since I knew there *was* a facility, but now it's even more important.

Georgette turns her bloodshot, droopy eyes on me. "You mean you don't know?"

I shake my head. "Should I?"

"Yes. It was your mama who helped create it."

My ears start ringing. I blink. Frown. "What did you say?"

"Your mama used to work for Cland Industries— the company responsible for creating the very first fully functioning, artificially intelligent robot. And later on, the ThinkChip, and its emergency backup system—your facility. You gain entrance to the facility,

you can take control of every ThinkChip in existence."

My mouth drops open. I try to make sense of everything Georgette just said—Ratch wants to control all ThinkChips, my mom helped create robots—but it's too much to process at once. My brain feels like a strawberry mashed up in a blender. I can't think straight, so all I manage to say is, "That's not true."

Po walks into the kitchen. I look over at him. I expect him to take my side, to tell Georgette she's cracked. But he doesn't. Instead he gives me that look of his that means he's got a big fat secret. One that he's feeling guilty for keeping.

"Trout," he says.

"Is it true?" I ask him.

He exhales and shuffles his feet. "Yeah."

"How come you and Dad didn't tell me?"

"Because Dad was waiting for the right time."

I curl my hands into fists. "When? When I'm fifty years old?"

My teeth grit against each other and I leap from the table. I march past Po without giving him a second glance. I don't want to be mad at him. It sorta feels like I'm being a baby about it, and heat rushes into my cheeks as I instantly regret storming out of there.

He calls after me once, but he doesn't follow, and I

think he knows that I just need a second to go over the new information.

I find a quiet, empty space in the back of Georgette's house and curl up, letting the anger wear off. I don't know how long it takes—maybe an hour. Maybe two. And in that time, I realize, just like Marsi said, that I can't blame Po for everything. Dad should have been the one to tell me about Mom. Po was just trying to follow Dad's orders.

Fact is, though, no one talks about Mom, and now I'm starting to realize just how much I *don't* know her. What else did she do before I was born? Did she ride hoverboards? Did she like climbing as much as I do?

What would she do if she were here now?

Even though I didn't know her, I bet when she helped make the first bot, she wanted them all to be good. Which makes me wonder again how any bot can become good or bad. Bots are more like humans than we think. Not all humans are good either, and there are a million different reasons why they become the way they are.

I think about Ratch in the factory, watching his friend Mel die in his arms. I think I'm starting to understand him a little bit more.

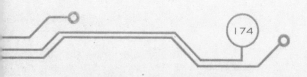

NINETEEN

I COME CRAWLING OUT of the hole I hid in and find Po right away beside Marsi's bed.

He's hunched over on his chair, elbows on his knees, staring at Marsi like he can make her wake up with the power of his brain.

"Hey," I say.

He jumps. "Hey. I didn't hear you come in."

I shrug. "I didn't want to disturb you."

"It's cool."

I come around the bed and sit in the other chair in the corner. I try real hard not to look at Marsi, because I don't want to remember her this way, weak and injured. I want to remember her as the happy, smiling Marsi.

"Sorry about earlier," I say, keeping my voice low. "I'm okay now."

Po raises his eyebrows. "Was that an apology?"

"Yes." I sigh. "You don't have to be a jerk."

He chuckles. "I'm not. Well, okay, maybe a little."

We sit there for a minute, then Po says, "If you ever want to talk about Mom, just say the word, okay? I've been keeping Dad's secrets for a long time." He sighs. "I'm not saying Dad is wrong, but when it comes to Mom, I want you to know everything from now on. You have the right to know her."

"Thanks." I pause. "Do you miss her? Mom?"

"All the time." He rests his head on the back of his chair. "When she was pregnant with you, her and Dad were redoing one of the bedrooms for you. She picked out a gray color for your walls. Dad spent an entire weekend painting the room. Then Mom decided it was too much like a prison cell, so then she did blue and said it was too sad. I remember her and Dad arguing about it, because he was tired of painting.

"So I got this grand idea to help them, and I got my crayons out and colored all over the walls."

Po lets out a laugh. "Dad was mad. Like spitting mad. Mom made him leave. 'Take a walk, Robert. I got this handled.' I thought Mom was going to take my toys away or something. Or ground me. Instead, she picked up one of my crayons and drew a turtle on the wall. I just stood there like an idiot until she looked over at me and said, 'Come on, Mason. Let's finish what you

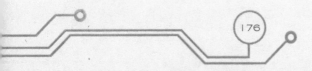

started.' She never, ever got mad at me. Like, she didn't have an angry bone in her body.

"When Dad came home, he just shook his head and grabbed a crayon and started drawing. It was hard to stay mad when you were around her."

I've never heard that story before. And Dad said we moved right after Mom died, so I was too young to remember the room.

"I wish you could have known her," Po says. "You know . . . like *really* known her. She was amazing."

After a minute, Po reaches over and pats my arm. "At least we got each other, ya? Where would I be without my weetle Trout?"

I grunt. "Ha. Ha. It's not like I've got anything special about me, though."

"Oh, little bro." He gets up, shakes out his leg, and starts hobbling out of the room. "Someday you're going to realize just how special you are."

I find LT sitting on Georgette's roof.

"How'd you get up there?" I call to him.

"There is a rain collection barrel on the southwest side of the house. I used it to hoist myself up."

I go up the same way and sit next to LT, arms folded around my knees. "Hey," I say.

"Hello."

The sky is a knot of dark clouds. The air smells wet and heavy.

"Marsi looks like she's doing better," I say after a minute of silence.

"Yes. Her heart rate is returning to normal. I can hear it even now. She will be fine. I am confident."

"That's good. Po's worried, you know."

"I know."

We watch an owl zoom past. LT turns to me when the bird is out of sight. "I overheard your conversation with Georgette and Po."

"About Ratch's clone army?"

LT makes a noise that sounds like a snort. "Yes, but that is not what I was referring to. Perhaps we can discuss Ratch's overzealous plans for world domination at a later date."

I laugh, even though it's not really that funny when you think about it.

"I meant the conversation about your mother and father," LT continues. "Specifically, about the facility. Now that you know what is inside it, I feel it is time I tell you everything. Particularly how, exactly, Ratch and I came to save your father."

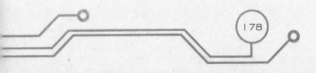

"Okay." I get a knot in my chest that tells me maybe this isn't good news. "I'm listening."

"When the war first broke out, robots worried the UD would use the ThinkChip facility to dismantle us. It was a realistic possibility. Thankfully, the government lost control of New York quickly, so they were unable to reach it. Ratch and I formed a plan: Find out whatever we could about the place. If we could reach it first, then we would be safe.

"We knew Robert St. Kroix was serving in the military, and wondered if perhaps he knew more information about the facility. Despite confidentiality, and security protocol, we knew it was probable a wife would divulge certain information to her husband. Information we needed.

"Your father was the easiest target to reach without compromising ourselves."

The owl hoots from its perch in a far-off tree. I sit up straighter and avoid looking at LT. "You saved Dad only because of the ThinkChip facility."

"Yes."

I take a deep breath. I know I should be questioning whether or not LT can be trusted, whether he's *really* my friend, but he has proven himself more than once.

Ratch never did anything to pretend he was my friend. He wasn't even nice half the time.

But more importantly, someone is finally being honest with me, without me having to question them first. In some ways, I think I might be able to trust LT more than anyone. LT is good with the truth. He doesn't keep it locked away forever and ever.

"You guys didn't injure Dad on purpose, did you?"

"No. We found him near death. Perhaps the reasons we saved him were ill intentioned, but it was one of the best things I have ever done."

"And when he woke up? Did he know any of the information you wanted?"

LT swivels his head no.

"You could have killed him then," I say.

"We could have."

"But you didn't. Why?"

LT shrugs. It isn't a gesture I see him do often. "I liked him. I suspect even Ratch liked him. And when the people of Line Zero learned about him, they were in awe. Your father was a good way to bridge the gap between humans and robots. I only wish Ratch would have accepted him. We would not be in this position if he had."

"Why didn't he?" I ask, thinking of the same question

I thought of earlier, the one that started the argument between Vee and me. "What makes Ratch different from you?"

"We are all a product of our environment, and Ratch's environment put him on a course much different from my own."

Mel, I think. And the factory where they worked. Humans made him the way he is now, I realize.

"We made him a villain," I whisper.

LT looks away. "It is more complicated than that. But in some ways, yes. Though you, specifically, are not at fault. It was the government. The corruption. The factory foremen. It was a lot of things."

I can't help but wonder where we would be now if Ratch hadn't watched his good friend die in a factory, in his arms.

If Mel had been given the upgrade she'd needed, would I be sitting here with Ratch right now instead of LT?

It's a lot to think about, but maybe it's not so far from a possibility. And if not, maybe there is still some good left inside Ratch.

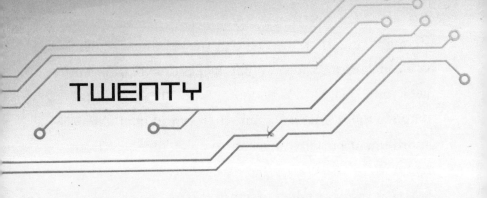

TWENTY

DAD CALLS PO'S Link just after ten that night to let us know he's safe. I'm so relieved, I feel like a weight has been lifted off my shoulders. We agree to stay put until Dad calls again with an update.

I call Lox after that, to let him know I'm okay, seeing as how he probably saw the attack on the news feed.

"Sweet mother of toads," he says when he sees me. "I thought you were space dust!"

I laugh. "I'm okay. I wasn't in Line Zero when the attack happened."

Lox frowns. "Where were you, then? Getting your hair done?"

"No, gearbox. I was with Tellie."

He bats his eyelashes. "Oooooh Tellie. I love you!"

"Shut up."

"Hey, you know how they used to combine celebrity couples names back in the old dusty days?"

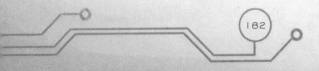

"Yeah."

"Well, get this. If you combine Trout and Tellie you get Trollie! Ha! Ding! Ding! That's like the best couples name in the history of couples names and mankind!"

I check the kitchen to make sure no one heard that, since we're on speaker. I'm still alone. "We are not a couple, Lox!"

"Yeah. Yeah." He waves at the Link like he's swatting a fly. "You say that now, but when you are, I'm using Trollie. I'm using it and you can't stop me."

We chat for a few more minutes before Tellie comes into the kitchen to let me know Marsi is awake. I say good-bye to Lox and promise to call him tomorrow.

Tellie opens the fridge. "I thought I'd make Marsi something to eat. You want to help?"

"Sure."

We warm up some soup for Marsi, and since Po has been glued to her side all day, and hasn't eaten much, I make him a veggie sandwich.

Ten minutes later, we carry the tray into Marsi's room. She's sitting up in bed, a sheet tucked around her midsection. She smiles when she sees me and eagerly takes the soup. "The St. Kroix brothers are my saviors."

I beam at her.

"Are you feeling better?" Tellie asks Marsi.

"Much. Thanks to all of you. I'll be up on my feet—"

"Everyone quiet." LT hovers in the doorway and holds up his hands.

We all go totally deadly still.

"What's wrong?" I ask, but he shushes me.

He looks out the window. I follow his line of sight, but with the lights on in Marsi's room, and the darkness beyond the windows, all I can see is our reflection in the glass, my panicked expression. My heart ca-thuds in my chest.

"Are you expecting anyone?" LT asks Georgette.

"No."

He glances at Linda. "Do you hear it?"

"I do."

"Is that a normal night sound for this area?"

"No. Never heard that one before."

My mouth is suddenly so dry, it's like my tongue is made of hay. A shiver creeps up my back.

I hear it now too. We all hear it.

It's a roaring. A screeching. A churning of gears.

And then the front of Georgette's house rips away in a crunching of wood and shattering of glass.

Po leaps onto Marsi's bed, covering her with his body. LT grabs me and rips me toward the kitchen.

"Tellie!" I scream. "Get Tellie!"

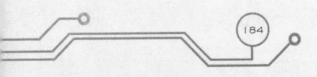

He sets me down and zooms back into the room as more of the house is torn away. It's like we're in the middle of a tornado, but instead of blowing the house to bits in one gust, it's taking it apart piece by piece, one giant bite at a time.

The roof groans and tears away from the walls. I huddle near the table, arms wrapped around my head as wood and shingles rain down on me. Dust collects in the corners of my eyes, coating my teeth in a gritty layer.

I chance a look, and there, silhouetted against the half-moon, are at least five tentacles. Metal tentacles with wires racing in and out of port holes.

One of Ratch's machines. I just know it.

When LT returns with Tellie, and Po comes in behind them with Marsi in his arms, my knees turn to rubber. "Where's Georgette?" I have to shout to be heard over the tearing and shattering of the house.

"Get out of the house!" Po yells as he blazes past me.

"Get Georgette! We have to get her out first!"

I take off down the hallway, or what's left of it. Marsi's room, where I last saw Georgette, is nothing but a broken floor and flipped-over furniture. "Georgette!" I shout into the gloom.

"Here," Linda calls.

I duck beneath a fallen ceiling board, climb over the bed, and find Georgette trapped in the corner, beneath a dresser. "My arm is pinned," she says, her voice totally calm. If I were her, I would be gearing out. "Linda and I can manage. You go on. Get to safety."

I shake my head. "I'm not leaving you. It's Ratch. Don't you see? He's here for you."

"Your life is more important than mine," she says after a grimace. "If he's here for me, he won't spare you, son." Her eyes pinch at the corners. "You understand what I'm saying?"

I do. She means Ratch might kill me, because I'm not worth much. But I don't care. A good leader doesn't leave a person to die.

I go around to the other side of the dresser. "Linda, can you push and I'll pull?"

"Yes. On the count of three?"

"On the count of three," I repeat. "One. Two. Three."

With Linda's robot strength, and my grunting and determination, we're able to move the dresser enough so that Georgette can slide out from beneath it. She slowly rises to her feet, cradling her arm at her side.

Linda steers her toward the back of the house, the only part still intact. We make it only five feet down the hallway when Ratch appears.

Linda puts herself between him and Georgette and me. "You'll have to go through me first," she says.

"Gladly." In a blink, Ratch is in front of us, inches from Linda's face. He reaches out with one hand and bats Linda aside like she's nothing more than a child's toy.

She slams into the wall and slides down it, coming to rest on the floor.

Now it's just me between Ratch and Georgette. My guts wheel around, like I'm on a roller coaster, like I might spill my last meal right there on the floor.

"Humans are inferior when it comes to strategy," Ratch says. "I could crush you before you took a breath, Trout. And you . . ." He turns to Linda as she climbs to her feet. "You're a decade old and you smell like burning rubber."

"I take defense to that!" Linda says.

Ratch snorts. "And if either of you had stopped to consider all possible ways I could take Georgette, then you wouldn't have put your back to her."

Linda and I whirl around just in time to see a gigantic tentacle snake into the hallway and snatch Georgette right off the ground. She lets out a stuttering screech. Linda leaps after her, but it's too late. Georgette is already fifty feet in the air, well out of our reach.

The tentacle retracts and Georgette's screams fade into the darkness.

There's a rustle behind me, a crunching of metal. I turn back around to find Ratch dangling from the end of LT's arm.

"Hello, brother," Ratch says, his voice filled with machine static.

LT growls. "We are no longer brothers."

"I know you're mad. I expected you would be, but I can't stop it now. You might as well kill me."

LT slams Ratch up against the wall. It crumbles from the force, and because there isn't much of it left anyway, it teeters back and forth.

"Do it," Ratch says. "Come on."

LT's fingers constrict. Something in Ratch's neck cracks. My chest grows light with triumph and apprehension. LT's going to end this now, once and for all. We've won.

Ratch chuckles, and wraps his hand around LT's wrist. "You can't do it. You have too many human emotions and attachments. You become more and more like them every day."

"You say that like it is a bad thing." LT cocks his free hand back in a fist. His gears wind up.

But just as LT throws a blow, Ratch jams up with his

knee, hitting LT in the torso. Something hisses. Smoke curls in the air. Ratch wrenches out of LT's grip, twists LT's arm around, and tears it from his body.

I suck in a gasp as LT drops to his knees.

"Face it, brother," Ratch says. "You're destined to be part of the heap if you stay on this side of the war. I beg of you, don't make me choose."

"You already have," LT answers.

Ratch grits his metal teeth. "So I have." He tosses LT's arm, still smoking and sparking, to the floor, and storms past Linda and me, disappearing in the woods just as quickly as he came.

TWENTY-ONE

FOR THE SECOND time in less than twenty-four hours, we're setting up an operating room. But this time it's LT getting fixed.

One lone bulb glows in the back of Georgette's old garage. It's the only part of her property not torn to bits. LT lies on a workbench, the wood splintered and weathered light gray. Linda is hunched over him, inspecting the damaged wires and metal bones in his shoulder socket.

"Hmm," she says, and clucks. "I think we can repair this, but it'll be a crude repair. And he might not have function in all his tentacles."

"Fingers," I translate.

"Right," Linda says.

I hand her a screwdriver and she gets to work.

"You doing okay?" I ask LT.

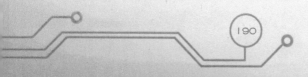

He chuckles. "Yes. Linda kindly shut off my touch sensors. I do not feel a thing."

In the far corner, Po has Marsi situated on a beach lounge chair, a red wool blanket spread over her legs. "How are you?" Po keeps asking her. "Do you need anything?" To which she replies, every time, "I'm fine, Po. Stop gearing out."

"Retti Torch, please," Linda asks. She points to a long golden stick on the workbench with a blue handle. Tellie reaches it before me and hands it to Linda.

And so it works like that for the next half hour, Linda requesting tools that Tellie and I fetch. When she's done, LT's arm is reattached, but it hangs crooked from his shoulder, and his index finger is missing.

"Try to move all your fingers," Linda says.

LT holds his hand up and three fingers wiggle together. The last, his thumb, bends forward at an odd angle, and creaks as it does.

"Good enough," LT decides, and hops off the table. Several metal shavings rain down from his repairs and plink against the floor.

Linda waves her hand in the air. "Don't worry. You didn't need those."

LT glances over his shoulder at Po. "Can she travel?"

"No way," Po answers at the same time Marsi says,

"Yes. I'm not broken." Po frowns at her. She scowls. "I'm fine, Po."

"You're not fine."

"Well, we can't stay here, now, can we?" she counters. "So I don't know what our other options are."

"We can go back to Line Zero," Po says.

"But you said Dad said not to come back unless he called," I point out. Po gives me a *shut up* look, but I ignore it. "Besides, we have to stop Ratch."

"And I have to save my dad," Tellie adds.

"No," LT says. "I will go after Ratch. If anyone should try to stop him, it should be me. And he has all the pieces he needs to break into the facility."

"You think Georgette would give up her code?" I ask.

LT leans against the table and his arm jolts like he's being hit with electricity.

I suck in a breath. "It's fine, it's fine," Linda assures me. "Just a short in his wires. No need to worry!"

"What I was about to say," LT goes on, "is that Ratch can be convincing when he needs to be. And if that does not work, he will resort to other means."

I gulp. I think he means Ratch will hurt Georgette, or maybe her daughter, the fashion designer in 1st District.

I hope it doesn't come to that.

"Then it's settled," Po says. "We're all going back to Line Zero. LT is going after Ratch."

Tellie takes a step toward the door. "You're not my boss. I'm not going back to Line Zero without my dad."

An amused smile spreads across Marsi's face, before she says, "I'm going too," and whips the blanket off her legs.

"Excuse me?" Po says to her. "You aren't—"

"Mason St. Kroix," she says, "if I want to help a girl save her dad, and stop a maniac robot from attacking the country, then I will. I don't need your permission."

I like Marsi more and more every day.

Po grumbles in the back of his throat. "You all have lost your gears."

I raise my eyebrows at him. "Does that mean you're coming too?"

"Well, I'm not going to let you go off by yourself. Dad would kill me." He goes to Marsi's side and puts his arm around her waist. "I still think this is a dumb idea."

"Sometimes dumb ideas turn out to be the best ideas," I argue.

Po snorts. "Yeah, but they probably don't entail possibly dying."

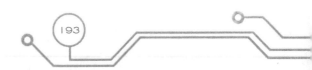

Err . . . that is probably true. So I keep my mouth shut after that.

We pack a few things, like food and medical supplies, and head out. LT, using his robot voodoo, figures out which way Ratch disappeared and leads us from Georgette's smashed house.

As we walk, Po tries calling Dad but gets no answer. A part of me worries that Po was right, and I was wrong, that we should have turned around and gone back to Line Zero. I know Dad was safe last we talked to him, but seeing him would make me feel much better.

I wish I could be in two places at once like Ratch and his clones.

"We should find a car, don't you think?" Linda asks LT. "We will never catch Ratch at this speed."

LT looks over his shoulder at her. "You are right. According to my mapping system, there is another town ten miles north of here. Perhaps I should go ahead to see what I can find."

We all agree that's probably a good idea, even though I haven't seen a hover rail since we left Georgette's. But I guess LT knows that, so maybe he'll look for a car that creates its own boost.

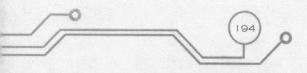

He salutes us good-bye and blazes off down the dirt road at the speed of a spacecraft, blowing up dust behind him in a gigantic cloud. I wave the air and cough. Tellie spits dirt out of her mouth.

We keep walking, and within a half hour, we hear the distant chugging of something. A machine, maybe.

Po snaps his fingers, getting our attention, and points to the woods. We leave the road behind, slinking through the trees as quietly as we can. I find a good spot between a bush and the thick base of an old tree and drag Tellie down beside me.

We watch the road as best as we can through a small break in the bushes. Headlights shine through the darkness. Tellie and I cower together, trying to make ourselves as small as possible.

The chugging gets closer. There's a loud whir of an engine. It's unlike anything I've ever heard before. It sounds ancient and broken.

And then it stops. Or at least, it stops moving, and quiets a fraction. The headlights wink out. Someone walks around the front of the vehicle and stops at the side of the road. Tellie shivers next to me, despite the fact that it's at least seventy-five degrees, and thick with humidity.

"It is I," someone calls.

I breathe a sigh of relief. "LT," I say. "Thank the universe."

All of us make our way out of the woods and stare at the vehicle—if you can even call it that. The first thing I notice, that makes my mouth hang open and my eyebrows pull together, is that it has wheels. Real wheels.

"This is like . . . a hundred years old!" I say. "Nothing moves on wheels anymore! Well, except for oldie bikes, but—"

"Shhh," Po says, and gives me a shove. "Maybe you want to flash a beacon light too? Let Ratch know where we are?"

"Whatever," I mutter, and circle the vehicle.

Rust has eaten away a lot of the car's body. One of the brake lights is smashed, the bulb missing. The other is hanging from its bracket like a loose tooth. The back window is completely gone and the front grill is smashed in.

But it's running. And there are enough seats for all of us. Plus LT apparently knows how to drive it, so I guess that's good.

Po helps Marsi into the backseat. She's slow moving, even more so than when we left Georgette's, and I can tell Po is worried about her. He gives her another pain

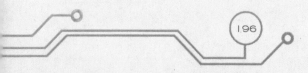

patch, one from Georgette's medi-kit, and within minutes she's sleeping.

Once we're settled in, LT puts the car in gear and it jolts forward, causing me to knock shoulders with Tellie.

"How long you think the trip will take in this thing?" Po asks.

"In manual mode, it will take approximately seventeen hours with no stops. If we can find a rail system somewhere between here and ONY, and a hovercar, we could cut the time down to nine hours."

"Then let's make that our mission," Po says.

For once, things go our way. We find working hover rails in a town called Charlotte and LT manages to "borrow" a hovercar from a large parking garage. I know I should feel guilty for being involved in a carjacking, but I'm more worried about Ratch.

As we drive through downtown Charlotte, I notice something that I haven't noticed in any other town. There are more robots than humans.

Here, the streets are alive and packed with figures, but the sun glints off more metal than I can stand to look at. I wish I had a pair of sunglasses.

"This is so notched," Tellie breathes. "I've gone from

seeing no robots to all of a sudden being surrounded by them." She rubs her arms. "It's a weird feeling."

"I'm used to robots, and even I feel weird here."

"It is because you are a minority," LT answers. "It is called the minority paranoia. We saw it a lot in robot factories, where robots far outnumbered humans. I imagine that only fed the eventual disputes between both humans and robots."

Tellie shivers. "Well, I don't like being a minority."

"No one ever does," LT answers over his shoulder.

Once we leave Charlotte, and connect to a free rail, LT programs the car to top speed. Pretty soon we're zooming toward Old New York. And the closer we get, the faster my heart thumps beneath my ribs, making it harder and harder to breathe.

I have no idea what we'll find in ONY. Will it be like Line Zero? With shops and humans and robots all together? Or will it be more like the machine wasteland I grew up picturing?

I'm scared to think of the possibilities.

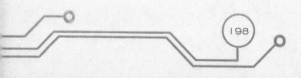

TWENTY-TWO

I WAKE A FEW hours later to the sound of Po whispering to LT. Po is sitting next to me, close enough that I can sorta hear what he's saying, if I strain real hard. So I keep my eyes closed and listen.

"He'll probably be expecting us," Po says, and LT confirms with a grunt. "We should be prepared."

"We will be."

I feel the car follow a curve in the road and tighten the muscles in my legs so I don't slide into Po.

"And furthermore," LT adds, "I know Ratch. And Ratch knows me. He will assume I will enter Old New York through some rarely used route. So I suggest we do the exact opposite and take the free rail straight into the city."

"By choosing the obvious, we do the unexpected," Po says. "I like it. How far out are we?"

"Two hours."

At that, my heart starts ka-thumping in my chest. We're only one hundred twenty minutes away from confronting Ratch. And what exactly are we going to do when we find him?

An hour later, the vid screen in the dash of our borrowed car flickers on.

"You do that?" Po asks LT.

"No." LT turns to Linda. "Did you?"

"It wasn't me," she answers.

At first the screen is blank, but then a vid feed starts rolling.

Ratch appears.

He's sitting in front of a row of windows and behind him, rain pelts the glass. The sky is dark and thick with clouds. I can't make out any of the background, so I don't know exactly where he is.

LT answers as if he read my thoughts. "It's raining in Old New York right now."

"Good afternoon," Ratch says to the camera. "I have a special announcement, which will be particularly important to those of you listening who happen to be robots or in possession of robots. I suggest if you're human, you get far, far away.

"In approximately ten minutes, all ThinkChips will

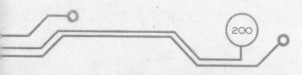

be in my command. And yes, that means *all robots* will be in my command. I'm sure you know what that implies. Just as World War I was not the end, Bot Wars I will not be either. I'm prepared to start Bot Wars II, unless you comply with what I ask of you."

LT pulls the car over and shuts the engine off.

"Ten minutes?" Tellie echoes. "That's not enough time to respond to demands."

"Exactly," Po says. "He doesn't want the demands met. He wants a reason to invade."

Tellie and Marsi, who woke a half hour ago, are crammed in beside Po and me, watching the vid over our shoulders.

Ratch goes on. "These are my demands . . . " He moves closer to the camera. I swear his band of eyes glows brighter. "First of all, I want Bot Territory declared a separate country, once and for all. I want Sixth District, and total control of the Science Institute stationed there. I also want the fence separating Bot Territory from the United Districts.

"Secondly, I want the military zone abolished, and all citizens of the United Districts are hereby banned from Bot Territory unless given permission by me to enter.

"And thirdly . . ." He cocks his head to the side,

pauses. I freeze. "I want any known human member of the Meta-Rise turned in to me immediately. If the members are not turned in to me, he or she harboring said members will be arrested.

"Anyone who turns in a member of the Meta-Rise or reports information on suspected members and their locations, will be awarded five thousand creds."

I look at Po. Po looks at me. We're all at risk of being turned in. We all have connections to the Meta-Rise.

"If you have information to report, call this number," Ratch says, and a Link number flashes on the screen.

"You have approximately eight minutes remaining to respond to my demands. If you have any questions," Ratch adds, "keep them to yourselves."

The screen goes black.

LT whips his door open and scrambles out of the vehicle. Po and Linda leave the car to follow.

Tellie slides in next to Marsi, who is still groggy, and pale. "I'll stay with Marsi if you want to go check in with your brother."

I nod a thanks and climb out of the vehicle. I don't know where we are—I wasn't paying attention when Ratch's vid came on—but now that I look around, I realize we're surrounded by the remains of an old neighborhood. There are houses crammed in next to

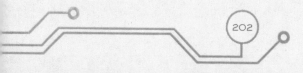

each other, with only a few feet between them. They're all a different shade of brown or white or gray, and their shutters, what remains of them, are either burgundy or forest green or black.

It might have been a fun place to live back when people were here, but now it just looks like a sad ghost town made out of caved roofs and overgrown hedges and cracked driveways.

I find LT, Linda, and Po standing at the end of a driveway in front of a gray house. "So what do we do?" Po asks. "If Ratch turns on the emergency backup, then he can make you do anything he pleases."

LT paces. "When we first learned that Ratch was trying to gain access to the facility, Scissor and I thought it was a smart idea to protect ourselves, and our operating systems, from outside influence. She developed an alternate ThinkChip, similar to what is used today, but they operate on a different frequency."

"So, you're safe, right?" I ask as I sidle in next to Po.

LT shakes his head. "We didn't have time to test it. It may not work." He stops pacing and looks right at me. "It is risky to allow my ThinkChip to remain. Linda and I should relinquish ours."

"What? No, LT! You won't be yourself if you don't have your chip."

"And if Ratch has opened the facility like he has claimed to, then I will not be myself anyway. Do you have any idea how much danger you will be in if Ratch has control of all of us? He will use our system to scan the vision of every robot in the country, and he will know right where you are located. I cannot be the reason you are harmed."

"It does sound as though you're in a cucumber," Linda says.

"A pickle!" I shout, and then immediately regret yelling at her.

"It's the best plan we got," Po says, and pops open the panel in LT's back. I guess that's where the ThinkChip is located, though how he knew that, I don't know.

He starts rooting around inside.

"Hurry," LT says quietly. "According to Ratch's given time, you only have one minute before he commandeers all robots."

Po tips his head toward me. "Will you get Linda's chip?"

Linda turns around without arguing.

"What am I looking for?" I ask.

"It'll be behind the spinal system. You'll feel a thick cord. Pry open the panel there and feel around inside the cord for a small box. It'll be the size of a teaspoon.

Once you locate it, pry it out. But be careful not to damage the cord. They'll lose all mobility if you do."

"Oh great," I mutter as I hunch to see inside Linda's back.

"Twenty-two seconds," LT warns.

Po grunts, grits his teeth. I can't see his hand, it's so far inside LT's back. "Got it," he says, and pulls out the box containing the ThinkChip. LT goes still.

"You didn't break him, did you?" I ask.

"Of course not," Po answers, and moves to help me. "Step aside."

Sweat beads on my forehead. I don't think we have much time left.

Po takes my place. He reaches inside Linda. "She's an older model," he says. "Bigger ThinkChip. Lower in the spinal system."

"How do you know all this stuff?" I ask.

"I have a stash of robot manuals in my bedroom."

"Since when?"

"Since forever." He grimaces and snatches his hand back. Blood wells in a cut on his finger. "Crap. I can't reach it. My hand is too big." He waves me over again. "Get in there. I'll walk you through it."

"But . . . what if . . ."

"Now, Trout!"

I shove my hand deep inside Linda's back, fingers tangling into wires. "I don't know what I'm looking for!"

"It's a box! The size of a—"

"Teaspoon, I know. But wher—"

Linda swings around, catching Po and me off guard. I stumble behind her, my arm still stuck in her robot innards. She swings a fist at Po. He ducks. She swings again.

LT just stands there and does nothing.

I wrench my arm back and fall to the cement, hitting my tailbone. Pain shoots up my spine. I squeeze my eyes shut for a fraction of a second, just enough time for Linda to grab me by the shirt and haul me up right off the ground.

Marsi and Tellie spill from the vehicle. "Trout!" Tellie screams.

"Aidan St. Kroix located," Linda says in a scratchy, disconnected voice. Like she's nothing more than a toaster telling me my bread is done. "Mason St. Kroix located. Tellie Rix located. Marsi Olsen located."

She stares right at me, and even though I know it's not possible, that robot eyes are not a window to the other side of a connection, I swear I can see Ratch staring back at me.

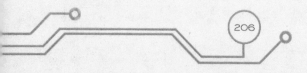

"How should I proceed?" Linda asks no one.

I struggle against her, punching her arms, her head, her chest. It's no use. She's a robot and I'm just a twelve-year-old boy.

"Proceed to Base 557290. Understood."

She whirls around and stomps off down the road, away from the car and Po and LT. She throws me onto her back and a torn sling pops out of a compartment in her shoulder, just like the one LT had in his old shell. The sling wraps around me.

I am so notched.

A sling means she's going to travel at mega warp speeds, and if she does, we'll be long gone in a matter of seconds.

I wrap my arms around her neck and squeeze. Po uses the headlock move on me all the time. I don't know what it'll do to a robot, considering robots don't have to breathe, but I have to try.

I clench my jaw, squeeze with everything I've got. Metal crunches, but not enough.

"Duck!" Po yells.

I have just enough time to let go of Linda and duck, when Po whacks her in the head with a rotted board.

The sling retracts and I spill out of it like goo.

Po swings again and Linda's head pops off like

the top of a dandelion and her body crumples to the ground.

I suck in a breath and lay my head on the ground.

"You okay?"

I open one eye and see Tellie hovering over me, her eyebrows knitted together in a look that I know means she's worried.

"Yeah. I'm okay." But really, on the inside, I'm worried I might barf.

Po, then Marsi appear in my line of sight. Sweat is running down Po's face. "Dude, I thought you were gone." He exhales with relief. "I guess that confirms it. Ratch has control of every—"

My Link buzzes in my pocket. Tellie helps me to my feet as I fish the Link out. Lox's name scrolls across the top.

At this point, he's the only connection I have to the UD, so I think his calling could be important.

I activate the call.

"What in fresh dung is going on?" Lox says when he appears onscreen. "The power just shut down and the city is going totally nuclear. I can hear people out in the streets screaming." He pushes aside the blinds and looks out the window. A second later, he jumps back and the blinds rattle as they settle.

"Sweet mother of tacos," he breathes, his cheeks turning ghost white.

"What?" I ask as everyone gathers around me to get a better look.

"It was . . . like . . . a . . . flying spider. Or something. Right past my window."

I glance at Po. "They're invading."

"And Ratch took control of the technological infrastructure," he adds. "Just like he did in Line Zero."

"Technological warfare," Tellie says, repeating the term her dad used when he addressed the UD after Ratch's last attack.

"This isn't good," Lox shrieks. "I'm too young to die! What if I die and come back as a robot? But like an ugly, useless robot, like a robot that scoops horse manure and composts it or something. Oh God, I am so screwed!"

"Lox," I say, shutting him up. "Just stay inside. Lock the house down. You'll be fine."

He puts his face just an inch from the Link screen, nostrils flaring. "NONE OF THIS IS FINE, BOLT-LICKER."

"Lox—"

"I'm going to die and return as a poop-eating robot." He throws his arm over his eyes as he collapses onto the couch. "I can't believe this is the end."

"Nothing is ending," I say. "I promise you that. We'll find Ratch and we'll stop him."

Lox peeks through his fingers at me. "Cross your heart and hope to die?"

"Yeah. Yeah. All of those things."

Something slams against the window behind Lox, startling him. "Mom!" he shouts. "I changed my mind! I want to move to Iceland now."

"Lox," she calls back. "Get in the basement this instant!"

"Gotta go," he says to me. "Get a move on saving the world again, FishKid. Time is running out."

The Link goes blank and I make a silent wish that Lox will be okay after this is all done.

"Now what?" Marsi asks the group.

Po sets his hands on his hips and looks past us, at the empty neighborhood, as he thinks.

I glance at LT. His back is to us. He's just standing there near the curb staring at nothing. Just like the houses are empty, so is LT.

It makes my chest hurt just thinking about it. What if he can never go back to being LT?

"If Ratch already has his codes . . ." Tellie says, and trails off. What she doesn't say is that, if Ratch has the codes, then he no longer needs her dad.

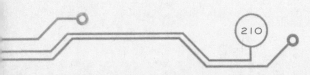

Marsi puts her arm around Tellie's shoulder and squeezes. "We'll save him, sweetie. I know we will."

Tellie wipes at her eyes.

"We have to figure out a way to get inside that facility," Po says. He runs his hand through his hair, then smoothes it back down.

"I bet we don't even make it into Old New York without being detected," Marsi says. "We have to come up with some kind of back-door entrance to the city."

I glance at LT again and a light winks on in my head. Somehow Po knows what I'm thinking too before I even say it.

"No way, Trout! No jamming way."

"What?" Marsi asks, looking between Po and me.

Tellie shuffles next to me. "Spit it out, Goldfish."

"If we can't get into ONY undetected," I say, "maybe we should go in the obvious way, just like LT said."

The girls look at me, still blank in the face.

"We put LT's ThinkChip back in place and let him drag us in as prisoners."

TWENTY-THREE

TELLIE WAGS A finger in my face. "That's pretty much the most cracked plan I've ever heard, Trout!"

She's calling me Trout again, which means she's not being funny or nice. She means business.

"I think I have to agree with her," Marsi says. Her hair has come loose from its rubber band since we've been standing outside. A light breeze blows down the street, pushing the now loose hair back and forth in front of her face.

"It's the only plan we got," I say.

Marsi tilts her head to the side and sends Po a questioning look. "Are you considering this?"

Po's mouth moves, but no words come out, which I guess means he doesn't know what to say, though I think he knows the only answer is yes.

"Po?" she says.

He shrugs and lets out a sigh. "He's right. It's the only plan we have, but you and Tellie don't have to come with us. Ratch doesn't want you, he wants us."

"You think I'm going to leave you?" she asks. "At a time like this?"

"You can't come," he says.

She snorts. "Yes I can."

"You're still hurt."

"And you only have one leg."

Po doesn't say anything at first. None of us do, and then we all start cracking up at the same time, because Marsi is right. Out of all of us, Po and Marsi are the ones with the biggest problems—a bum leg and a bullet wound. But I get the feeling neither will hold them back.

"Fine," Po finally says, and looks at Tellie. "Do you want us to take you somewhere safer?"

She shakes her head, sending several pieces of hair flying into her face. "My dad is out there somewhere, and I plan on finding him."

"Then I guess we're doing this," Po says.

I nod. "I guess so."

Tellie and Marsi sit on the hood of our borrowed car. LT stands in front of Po and me, staring at us with his

blank, dead robot eyes. We had to tug on him, coax him along, just to get him to move away from the curb.

"All right," Po says, "here goes nothing."

My knees go light and airy, like I'm in zero gravity. My heart drums in my ears. This could go horribly, terribly wrong. And it was my idea.

Po pushes the ThinkChip in and I hear it click in place.

It's like we all take in a deep breath at once.

LT cocks his head to the side. Po shuts the panel and comes around front to face LT.

"LT," I say, playing along with our plan. "You okay?"

There is a moment where he does nothing but stare at us, a calculating expression on his face, like he's analyzing the situation. Like he's trying to figure out what is the best course of action. I can't tell if that's a good thing—maybe Scissor's upgraded ThinkChip worked?

But then he grabs me by the arm and squeezes. I have to grit my teeth not to yelp. Tellie gasps.

"LT?" I say again, frowning, acting the part. "Can you hear me?"

"It's not working," Po shouts, saying the exact line we decided he'd say. "Take the chip back out. Take it out!"

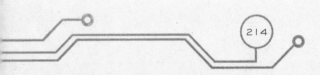

Everyone moves into action, but LT is faster, and grabs Po's arm. He drags both of us to the vehicle.

"Mason St. Kroix and Aidan St. Kroix located. How to proceed?" He whips open the back door and stuffs us inside. Po and I protest and the girls scramble in beside us, acting confused, just like we told them to.

If Ratch is watching on the other end, we want to make this as convincing as possible.

"Proceed to Base 557290, understood. En route now." LT starts the car up. The doors lock around us. Thump. Thump. Thump. We're trapped. The car pulls away from the curb.

None of us dares speak. LT has super-human hearing, and we must assume that whatever LT sees and hears, Ratch can too.

I settle against the seat, trying to trust in the fact that we're doing the right thing.

We pass an old freeway sign that says *New York City 38 miles.*

But instead of following the directions to take us into the city, LT veers off the freeway and takes us north.

That's probably not a good sign.

Po fidgets in his seat, then leans forward, elbows on

his knees. "I think LT's been fried," he says to me with a wink. "What should we do?"

"I say we make a break for it."

Tellie starts to say something when LT interrupts. "Anyone caught trying to escape will be eliminated on the spot."

My eyes widen with legit shock. I've never heard LT talk that way, and worse yet, I believe the threat. Because it isn't LT anymore, it's Ratch. And I think Ratch is willing to do just about anything to get what he wants.

We sit in silence for a bit longer and watch the road go from crumbling freeway to well-kept hover rails that wind through hilly terrain and overgrown farmland. When LT veers off the main street onto a narrower road, Po's hands tighten into fists in his lap. I don't have much muscle to fight with, so I mentally flex my brain, knowing it's the only thing I've got that might help.

When the car's readout says we've traveled a quarter of a mile off the main road, the trees thin out, revealing an open field with a small, one-story brick building plopped in the middle. If I had come here on any other day, under any other circumstances, I wouldn't think much of the building. The bricks have been painted gray, the doors and trim white. There are only two win-

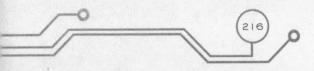

dows in the front, but for the size of the building, that seems like just enough.

Despite all that, like how small it looks, and how nondescript it is, the grounds surrounding the building . . . well, that's another story.

The place is swarming with robots. All shapes and sizes. I count six at first, but then I catch movement off to the left and see a short bot hidden in the trees far off in the distance.

Two bots, taller than Dad, with box-like heads and armored shoulders, guard the front door. Four more bots with thin, oddly bent legs pace the grounds. Another is positioned on the roof of the building, a large gun strapped around her midsection.

Two more bots approach our car, one on the driver's side, another on the passenger.

LT rolls the window down. "I have Mason and Aidan St. Kroix in my possession," he tells the bot at the driver's side.

The bot—a woman, from the sound of her voice— nods, and waves us through. "He's waiting for you and your prisoners below ground. Report inside and the guard there will escort you."

The second bot, the one on my side of the vehicle, bends over and peers inside. I shrink away from the window as its black, lifeless eyes stare at me, unblinking.

I know robots don't have to blink, but LT used to, just to make himself seem more human.

LT pulls the car up to the side of the building and parks. He gets out. None of us move as we wait for instructions. "No one do anything crazy until I say, got it?" Po whispers as LT comes around to the back.

"What if we can't get out of here?" I ask.

"We will. I promise. Just do as you're told and everything will be fine."

LT opens the back door. "Out," he orders. I scramble out.

We're led through the front door into a room with two chairs, a fake plant, and a bare end table. There's a set of elevator doors directly across from us. The doors open before any of us approach.

"Inside," LT says, and we pile in. There are only four buttons on the control panel. Level 1. Level 2. Level 3. And lastly, California. All of them are below ground.

I don't know what that means, having one floor named after an old state, but I think it must mean it's an important level.

LT picks Level 3 and the doors whoosh shut.

It only takes the elevator 1.5 seconds to reach its des-

tination. When the doors open, Tellie latches on to my arm like a spider monkey.

Level 3, from what I can see, is a lab run by what I can only describe as clone robots—*Ratch* robots. They're all exactly the same height (somewhere around Po's six feet), and all are made of a flat, black composite, so that the glare of the ceiling lights seems to ignore them, bouncing off the metal surfaces of the desks and the polished floor, but not the bots.

There must be somewhere between twenty and thirty of them. They hurry around the room with purpose, some manning computers, others watching the row of monitors attached to the wall on the right. Footage from all around the country plays on the monitors, and what I see is total chaos.

Robots, everywhere. In 1st District, on the beach. In 3rd District, on the desert. In 4th District, on the floating island cities in Lake Michigan. And 5th District, right in the center of downtown Brack.

The main screen shows the capitol. There are robots surrounding a darkened Congress Hall. The billboards atop the other buildings are blank. Ratch really did take over all the power in the UD. I wonder what happened to the power in Bot Territory, in Line Zero.

Rows and rows of soldiers carrying rifles and laser pistols face hoards of robots.

It's a stand-off of the most epic kind.

I'm pretty sure I know who will win if they start fighting. The robots look way scarier than the soldiers, and the robots can withstand far more damage.

"This way," LT says, and leads us through the workroom, through a gray door, down a hallway, and finally into an office the size of three of my bedrooms back at home. More monitors hang from the walls here, but all of them are off.

Ratch stands behind a long metal desk, arms crossed over his chest. "LT," he says, and nods at his old friend. "Thank you for bringing them in. Report to California Level."

LT bows and disappears into the hallway.

Po shifts next to me. Either he's nervous, or his bum leg is hurting. Neither option is a good one. "Funny, you had to take away LT's freedom of thought in order to make him your friend again." Po narrows his eyes. "He won't ever, *consciously*, stand by your side."

Ratch's claw-like hands clench at his sides, and I think for a second he's going to hit Po. Instead, he yells, "Guards!" and summons four clone bots. They march

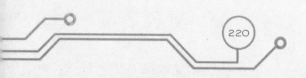

into the room, one for each of us. "Escort them to their cells."

The bot closest to me wraps his hand around my arm and drags me toward the hallway.

"Hey!" Po shouts, and wrestles against the bot, only to get a swift jerk of the arm.

"I suggest you cooperate," Ratch says behind us. "Wouldn't want you losing the other leg."

Po starts to argue when I knock him with my elbow. "Shut up," I whisper.

He grumbles in the back of his throat but shuts up real quick.

We're escorted back to the elevator and to Level 1. There we're dragged down several twisty, turny hallways, and finally to our cells, a separate one for each of us. Great. There's no way for us to communicate, since the cells are completely enclosed save for a tiny slit in the front of the doors. For our food trays, I guess.

I'm tossed in the first room, and the door is shut behind me, the lock bolted in place. I stand on the tip of my toes and peer out the small square window set in the door. I watch as Po, then Marsi and Tellie, are locked into their own cells. Marsi and Po are across the hall from me. Tellie goes in the cell to my left.

When the clone bots leave, Po presses up against his window and mouths something to me.

At first I don't know what he's saying. It takes him a couple of tries to get the message across.

We have to get out of here, he says. And I roll my eyes. It's not like I didn't know that.

But how? That's the question I don't know the answer to.

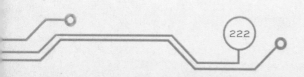

TWENTY-FOUR

I T SEEMS LIKE we sit in the cells forever. There are no TVs, or magazines, or books. Nothing but a bed, a toilet, and a sink. So I lie down, trying to think of ways to escape with nothing but a bed, a toilet, and a sink to help me.

Not surprisingly, I got nothing.

This has to be one of the stupidest ideas I've ever come up with. Po is probably cursing me right now.

I check the window in the door every now and then, but everyone else is either lying down, or tired of looking at an empty hallway, because I don't see Po or Marsi for a long time. I wonder what Tellie is doing next door and wish I could see her, just to make sure she's okay.

It isn't until hours later that someone comes to see me.

It's LT.

My cell door unlocks. He comes inside. He leaves the door slightly ajar.

"Have a seat," he says, and sits on the bed.

If he's still under Ratch's control, I don't know what he's capable of, so I stand there for a second staring at him while he stares at me.

"We have less than twelve minutes before the security override expires," he whispers. "Sit."

That time, he sounded more like the old LT, so I sit.

"Scissor's upgrade operates on a frequency similar to the old ThinkChips, so my control comes and goes. I am unsure of my time. So please, listen carefully. You have to dismantle Ratch. The *real* Ratch. Without his guidance, his clones will be no different from any other bot. They will not be as dangerous. The way to tell the real Ratch from the clones is by a piece of patched charcoal metal in the side of his neck. It was a repair I did on him while in the field during the Robot Wars. He never fixed it and it was an element he did not put into his clones.

"Secondly, when I am out, take my left arm. There is a universal key in the compartment there that Ratch had installed when I arrived. It will open all the doors in this facility. You will find Mr. Rix, Georgette, and Heather on Level Two. You will have to take three

turns to reach their holding area. One right, two lefts. Remember that."

"I can't," I say. It's all happening so fast. Too much information at once. "You should get Po. He's better at remembering stuff, you know. I'm just a kid—"

LT shakes his head once. "You are lighter and quicker on your feet. Your brother is strong, and smart, but he is at an extreme disadvantage with his leg. If someone should come in, you will at least have a chance of escaping."

A lump forms in my throat. "I can't, LT."

"Yes you can. Now, repeat after me. One right, two lefts."

I try swallowing the lump, but it stays in place. "One right, two lefts."

"Good. Now, in addition to that, your bag is waiting for you at the end of this hallway."

My bag, I wonder, but then I remember, I have one of Scissor's arthropods. LT must know about it. It could come in handy. Except, I only have *one*. I'm not sure what good it'll do me if I don't have enough for everybody.

"But . . ." I take a deep breath. "What do you mean, when you're 'out'?"

He opens the compartment on his right arm and

withdraws a syringe filled with green liquid. "This. It will shut down my system for a few hours. Hopefully long enough for you to dismantle the control server. I do not want to risk Ratch using me . . ."

His face goes still.

"LT?"

His fingers curl into claws and the needle drops to the floor. "I have little time left," he says. "Now! Get the syringe!"

I drop to the floor, scoop up the needle, and whirl around, jabbing it into LT's neck. I hit the plunger as his hand clamps over my wrist and bends my arm back. The needle goes skittering across the floor. LT picks me up with his other hand, slams me against the wall, and knocks all the air from my lungs. I gasp and gasp and gasp to get it back, but it's like I'm in water, drowning.

My eyes bug out. LT hoists me up, higher and higher, and just when I think I'm done for good, his hand loosens and I slide to the floor.

Air trickles into my lungs.

LT stumbles back. His metal eyelids shut, then flip open, then shut again.

I cram myself in the corner of the room when he

starts flailing all over the place. I make myself as small as I can, afraid that if he notices me, he might start gearing out real hard.

And then, suddenly, he goes slack, keeling over like a mushy banana. His eyes stay closed for good this time.

"LT?" I try, unsure of whether or not I want him to wake up. I don't want him to be dead, but I also don't want him smashing me like a bug.

When he doesn't respond, I crawl toward him and give him a nudge with my foot.

Nothing.

I burst into action, because I don't know how much time I have left before the security system comes back up. Probably not enough.

I push LT upright and pop open the panel in his torso. I start pressing the buttons there and random panels slide open, one on LT's leg, another in his thigh, then another between his shoulders. And finally I find the right button for the panel on his arm.

When it slides open, I peer inside. There are a jumble of wires, all with different connectors on the end.

I don't see a key anywhere.

I start picking through the wires, digging inside LT's arm, and then it dawns on me.

LT said *take my arm*. He didn't say, look inside my arm for a key, he said to take the whole thing.

The wires and connectors are the key.

Great.

Did LT really want me to take off his arm?

What other choice do I have? He's too heavy for me to carry.

My stomach swims as the seconds tick away in my head. I take a deep breath and try to give myself a pep talk.

You can do this, Trout.

He's just a robot. He'll get another arm. If he's okay, that is. If you didn't kill him with that serum.

He already lost one arm and had it repaired. What's one more?

I wrap my hands around his wrist, brace my foot on his stomach, and give his arm a yank.

Metal pops and crunches. The arm hangs loose by a few threads and bolts.

So I dig my foot into his stomach even more, clench my teeth together real tight, and yank one more time.

The arm comes free and I stumble back, hitting the floor on my tailbone. Pain shoots up my back and down my legs. "Oooooh," I moan, rubbing at the sore spot.

I get hold of myself, slowly rise to my feet and take

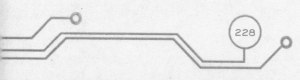

LT's arm with me. I try not to look back at him, at the empty arm socket, but I can't help it. He looks so sad and pitiful. Everything about him is wrong.

I just want my old friend back.

Carrying LT's arm with me, I go out into the hallway. Po is there at his door, glaring down at me. "What are you doing?" he asks, his voice muffled through the door.

"Saving your butt."

He snorts.

I find the main control panel near Po's cell. It opens with the press of my finger. The controls on the inside gleam bright red. There are a series of numbers along the top row, white buttons beneath those. Then a row of ports. There's a circular port, a rectangular port, then one with a flat bottom and rounded top.

Holding LT's arm between my legs, I sort through the wires in his compartment. The first couple of wires I grab are the wrong ones. I check several more, finally locating the circular port. I plug it in, and it fits perfectly. I find the rectangular port next, then lastly the flat-bottomed one. When they're plugged in, I hit all of the buttons, and one by one, the cell doors slide open with a rush.

Po is the first out of his cell, then Tellie and Marsi.

"Come on," I say. "We have to hurry up! The cameras will come back on soon."

I go to the end of the hallway and scoop up my bag. Po rushes past me and slowly pops open the door, peering out. "We're clear," he whispers, and ushers us through one by one.

"LT told me where to find Mr. Rix and—"

"My dad is here?" Tellie asks, and her eyes immediately fill with tears. "Is he okay?"

"I don't know. LT didn't say. They're all on Level Two. Mr. Rix, Georgette, and Heather Evans, from Fourth District."

"Getting down there is going to be hard," Po says.

"But we have to," I point out, and he nods.

"LT say if there was an alternate way down? Like stairs?"

"He didn't, but I bet there are. It's, like, mandatory isn't it?"

"In a place like this? No idea." He looks past me down the darkened hallway. "Come on."

We follow him around a curve in the hall, then take a left, then a right, and finally spy a stairwell sign at the very end of another hall.

Po is the first one inside. He looks down the well. "We're good."

Since we only have to go down one floor, the descent down the stairs doesn't take long at all. I take the lead this time, checking the hallway before waving everyone else in.

"Now where?" Tellie asks.

"We go right, then . . . oh crap."

"Oh crap what?" Po whispers.

"LT gave me directions, but they were directions for taking the elevator."

Po turns around and scratches at the back of his head. I think he's hiding all of the curse words he's muttering beneath his breath.

"Sorry!" I say.

"No, it's okay. We're okay." Marsi taps a plastic sign glued to the wall just outside the stairwell. "It's a map of the floor layout. We can figure out where we need to go using LT's directions. It's like doing a division problem instead of a multiplication."

"Yeah, she's right," Tellie adds, joining Marsi at the sign. "It's a piece of cake."

Po and I glance at each other. I think neither of us knows what the girls are talking about.

"What are the directions?" Marsi asks, using her finger to trace the route as I relay it.

"LT said, take one right, then two lefts."

"So, my dad is here," Tellie says, and plants her index finger on a hallway marked *2.5*.

"And we're here," Marsi says, pointing to the red dot that's supposed to represent our location. "So we need to go left, right, right."

Tellie smiles and her and Marsi give each other a high five. "Girls rule," Tellie says.

"Yes they do," Marsi replies.

"Then, lead the way, ladies," Po says with a grin.

When we reach the hallway we need, we find a hulking robot guarding the entrance. He's easily twice the size of me, which would put him at nearly ten feet tall. His shoulders are broad and sharp, his face nothing but a bubbled lens. Wires run in and out of his torso, pumping a sickly green liquid.

"Jam," Po breathes, and pushes us back before the bot spots us.

Tellie exhales. "We're so close."

"We need a distraction." Po gnaws at his bottom lip as he thinks. "If only I had a weapon." He turns to me. "What's in the bag?"

"Just some snacks and my arthropod."

Po furrows his eyebrows. "A what?"

"It's this thing that goes on my arm and creates its

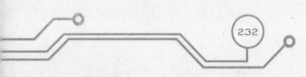

own hoverpoints, like . . ." I look up, my jaw dropping open. "I got a plan."

I hand Tellie LT's arm, then drop the bag to the floor and unzip it, pulling out the arthropod a second later. I remember exactly how Scissor taught me to open the contraption, how to slide my arm in, then close it.

"What's it do?" Po asks. "What's your plan?"

"You'll see."

"No, I don't want to see. I want you to tell me before you end up dead."

I go to the end of our hallway, ignoring him. I plant my feet for a running start. "Back up," I mouth, waving them aside. They press themselves into the wall.

I take off at a sprint, pumping my arms at my sides. I round the corner into the next hallway and the robot immediately squares himself in a fighting stance, ready to take me on.

The gun on his forearm starts spinning, charging itself up.

"Trout! Get out of there!" Po yells.

I count to three, waiting for the split second before the robot shoots.

One.

Two.

I whip my arm up and hit the button on the inside of my thumb.

"Trout!"

Three.

A laser shot blasts from the gun. My hoverpoint zings out of the arthropod, lodging itself in the ceiling. My feet leave the floor. I fly through the air as the laser shot zooms beneath me.

The bot doesn't have a chance to collect himself.

I pick up momentum, arch my back, kick out my legs, and slam into the bot's torso with both feet.

He sails backward, turning in midair so he hits the floor on his side.

Po runs beneath me, leaps on top of the bot, and rips open the torso panel. He jams his hand inside and pulls a fist of wires out. Sparks snap through the air as the bot seizes up and fizzles out.

I detach the hoverpoint and hit the ground with both feet, sweat beading beneath my nose.

"That was so kila," Tellie says as she and Marsi come up behind us.

I wipe the sweat away with the sleeve of my shirt. "I'm glad it actually worked."

Po whirls around. "You mean you weren't sure?"

"Well . . ."

He growls and charges after me, but Marsi stops him with a hand on his chest. "It worked. That's all that matters. We should focus on rescuing Tellie's dad and Georgette."

"Agreed," Tellie says. She hands me LT's arm and pulls open the door behind us. She rushes inside the hallway, checking the tiny windows set into the cell doors.

At the third door, Tellie jumps up and down and shouts to me, "He's in here!"

I use LT's arm at the control panel and the cell doors open a minute later with a whoosh of air. Mr. Rix dashes out, scooping Tellie into his arms in a big hug. He twirls her around.

Next, Georgette comes stumbling out of her cell, and behind her a woman I recognize from the news feed—Heather Evans.

"Good to see you all," Georgette says. She nods at Heather behind her. "This is Ms. Evans. Ms. Evans, these are friends of mine."

She eyes us. "They're just kids."

"Clever, brave kids at that," Georgette adds.

"It's nice to meet you all," Ms. Evans says. "Though I wish it were under different circumstances."

"Nice to meet you too," I answer.

Po nudges me with his elbow. "How about we get out of here now?"

"Yeah, about that . . ." I start. "How *are* we getting out of here?"

"I can get us out," Georgette says. "This is an old research facility that Cland Industries used before the war. There's a tunnel off Level One that will take us two miles outside of the city to a warehouse we used for storage."

"How hard will it be to reach the tunnel?" Po asks.

Georgette shrugs. "I suppose that all depends on how many robots we run into."

"And when we get out," Po starts, "will you tell us the way to the facility where they're controlling Think-Chips?"

She nods. "I will."

"Then let's get out of here."

TWENTY-FIVE

WE MAKE IT to Level 1 quickly, but have to hide in a storage room as a group of bots marches past. One of them says something about the prisoners, about them escaping, and I know right away we're cracked if we don't get out of here soon.

When the hall is clear, we file out.

"Access to the tunnel is to your right," Georgette whispers, and stops us about fifty feet down the curving hallway. "Here." She nods at an unmarked door in the middle of the wall. "This is the one we want."

The door opens easily and I breathe a sigh of relief. I'm waiting for something to happen, for a robot to jump out at us. My dad used to say that if something is too good to be true, it usually means you are about to get yourself in trouble.

There are no lights on inside the tunnel, so Tellie and I hang on to each other, while I use my other hand to trail along the wall, following the shifting, twining stone.

I can't wait to be outside in the fresh air.

It's totally silent down here, save for the shuffling of our feet, and the in and out huff of our breath. It feels like we're climbing into the center of a tomb.

Finally, after what feels like hours, I see little pin-points of light in the ceiling. Red and green and yellow. Georgette leads us to the left. Po and Marsi are in the back, moving along at the pace they can manage. I know it's too slow, though. Po walks slow by normal standards. And Marsi is still healing.

I worry that neither of them has enough energy to make it to our final destination.

Even though it's dark inside the tunnel, I can tell instantly when the space widens. Our footsteps echo around us. It's colder too, and goose bumps stand on my arms.

"Keep straight," Georgette says over a shoulder.

I check to make sure Po and Marsi are still behind me. Po has his arm around Marsi's shoulders, and her head is hung low.

"Is she okay?" I call.

"She's fine," Po starts. "I think we just need to—"

A low humming noise fills the space around us, and

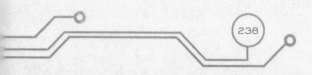

suddenly the cavernous room is blazing with light as one fixture after another flicks on.

Tellie squeezes my hand.

I freeze in place.

There, in the middle of the room, blocking our path to the other side, is Ratch. And he isn't alone.

He has a prisoner.

He has our dad.

I guess our escape *was* too good to be true.

I take a step toward Dad, but Ratch holds up a hand and shows me a little black device the size and shape of a remote control. "Come any closer," he warns, "and I'll press the button."

Po's fingers tense into fists. "What happens if you do?"

"Po, don't, please," Dad starts, and then Ratch presses the button.

Dad's robot hand curls into a fist, and his arm swings upward, catching him across the jaw. He stumbles back. He punches again, this time denting the metal plate in the side of his face.

"Stop!" I shout.

"That's what happens," Ratch answers.

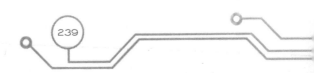

"He has control of Dad's robot parts?" I say to Po. "But how?"

"I gave him a ThinkChip," Ratch says. "Didn't have one until now. I think it's a vast improvement."

Po turns away from us, running his hand through his hair. He curses beneath his breath. Usually when he's like this it's because I left out the milk. I wish that was the case now. I can deal with that.

When Po turns back around, his jaw is clenched tight, so when he speaks, his words come out mashed together. "So what do you want? In exchange for our dad."

"Po," Dad says again, this time in his warning voice. But Po ignores him.

"Come on, metal head. Tell me your demands."

Ratch smiles. "All right. You made a speech after the bombing on Edge Flats. The one that made you a celebrity? Respected by many. Robots and humans. I want you to make another."

Po shuffles his weight around. Sweat rolls down his temples. Veins rise in his forehead. "What do you want me to say?"

"Address the Meta-Rise and Texas." Ratch takes two steps forward. "Tell them your dad and his team have been working on a tech patch. Tell them it was designed

to combat technological warfare. Tell them you worry there will be a second wave aimed at Bot Territory and Texas, particularly the areas heavy with human populations. And that, if they want their electronics and Net connections to be safe, they should download the patch immediately."

Po snorts. "So you can take over their electronics too?"

Ratch shakes his head. "That isn't good enough anymore. I don't want to control them. I want to shut them down. For good. How do you make a strong, defiant society come to heel? You take away everything they know and you refuse to give it back. You know what happens after that? Total chaos. Guess who will fix it?"

"You," I say.

Ratch laughs. "No. LT. They will trust him and I will control him."

Behind him, Dad plants his feet, grits his teeth. His hair hangs in his face, coated with dirt and sweat. Black circles ring his eyes, but determination is etched into the lines around his mouth.

He brings his machine arm up, points it at Ratch's back. His new upgrade shines in the light. The Raven Blast activates, the veins glowing orange, and a shot whumps out of the arm. The ground vibrates beneath me as the blast hits Ratch in the back, blowing him into a thousand twisted pieces.

For a second, relief floods through me. Dad stopped Ratch. We're safe. It's over.

Ratch is dead.

But then a door opens to our left and another Ratch—a clone—marches out.

I forgot about the clones.

"Excellent shot, St. Kroix," Ratch says, and pulls out a new remote, hitting a button.

Dad's face contorts with pain. He collapses to one knee and clutches at his heart. His skin turns bright red.

"Stop!" I turn to Po, desperate for something. "Make him stop!"

"Okay!" Po shouts. His shoulders level out. "I'll do it. I'll make the speech!"

Ratch lets go of the button. Dad pitches forward to both knees. He sways back and forth. "Son," he tries, but he has trouble staying upright.

"I have to do it, Dad. You would have done the same thing." Po grits his teeth. "Let's get this over with."

Ratch says, "Follow me."

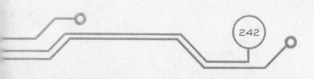

TWENTY-SIX

WE'RE ALL TAKEN back inside the building, out of the tunnel, and to the California Level. Dad is put in a chair, handcuffs placed around his wrists and latched onto a pipe behind him. Tellie, Marsi, Georgette, Mr. Rix, Heather, and I are told to sit in a row of chairs across from Dad, near the door. So we do. We're guarded by a tall bot with thin legs but bulky shoulders. There's a laser gun attached to his left arm.

Ratch leads Po into another room. Half the wall that separates us from him is made of frosted glass, so we can only see the movement of shadows on the other side until someone hits a button and the frost dissipates.

I see Po first. He's seated in front of a vid cam in the middle of the room, and sitting next to him, just out of sight of the camera, is President Callo. There are bruises beneath his eyes, and another along his jaw. His lip is crusted over with blood, and his hair, usually sprayed into a swoop over his forehead, sticks up funny on the side of his head, like he slept on it that way for days. When he sees us on the other side of the glass wall, hope flickers in his eyes.

There are two robots behind the camera, one standing guard, the other holding a SimPad. "This is your script," Ratch explains, and points at the pad. "We're recording, and we aren't live, so don't think you can warn everyone by veering off the script. This won't air until I'm satisfied it's done right."

Ratch crosses his arms and stands just out of the camera's frame. "Now, everyone quiet. We're recording in three . . . two . . . one . . ."

Po sits up straight, clears his throat. Ratch motions him to begin.

"People and bots of the Meta-Rise, citizens of Texas and Bot Territory, I come to you with an important message. In light of the recent attacks on the UD, we believe we're next in line for an attack. The terrorists known as the rogue robots from Old New York are looking to take over everything we've worked so hard to build. My father's tech team has created a patch designed to combat technological warfare. The patch will protect you and your electronics from Ratch's attacks.

"Download the patch immediately. There will be a

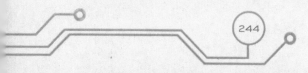

link posted below this vid along with instructions for the download and installation." Po puts his hand up in a fist. It's a gesture for the Meta-Rise. He says, in his most serious voice ever, "Rise from the heap."

The vid recording ends.

I let out a breath of relief. I was worried Po wouldn't do it. Or worse yet, that he would record the vid, but say something completely opposite of what Ratch wanted. And then he'd get himself killed.

Po's good at doing exactly the opposite of what people want him to do.

I watch as he stands up. He rocks his shoulders back, flexes his jaw.

Oh no.

I know that look.

Po lunges, grabs the vid camera tripod and cocks it back like a bat. He whacks Ratch across the head; Ratch's head pops off and his knees crumple. Po uses the leg from the cam stand to stab Ratch in the chest, sizzling his operating system.

The second bot in the recording room charges at Po. Po uses the tripod to hit the bot like a baseball. The bot flies into the windows separating us from them. The glass spiderwebs and caves outward.

The bot holding the SimPad cocks his fist back,

aiming it at Po. I scream his name, but at the last second, the president stands, hoists his chair over his head, and smashes the bot to the floor.

Po looks at Callo. "Thanks."

Callo nods. "Don't mention it."

The door next to me opens and three more Ratches enter the room.

"Run!" Po shouts. He shoves Callo toward us as he gears up for another round with a Ratch clone.

The bot guarding us lunges for me, but I dodge out of the way. Dad yanks at his handcuffs, but the metal doesn't give.

"Go, Trout!" Po says again. "Take the president to safety!"

Heather smashes her foot into the knee of Ratch #2 while Georgette kicks Ratch #3 to the floor. With a quick flick of her hand, she pops open his back panel and starts tearing out wires.

Dad braces himself and gives his cuffs another hard yank as the guard grabs a nearby chair and breaks it over Dad's head.

"Dad!" I scream.

Blood pours from his nose. The metal side of his face is so dented and scratched, I hardly recognize him.

I look around the room for a weapon, something to

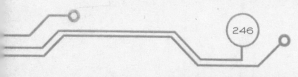

stop the bot from doing more damage, but there's nothing but a few more chairs and I know I'm not strong enough to use one as an effective weapon.

If only LT were here!

A hand clamps down on my wrist. Someone drags me back.

"Hey!" I flail and fight back till I realize it's Tellie. Mr. Rix and Georgette are waving us toward the exit with the president in tow, while Marsi and Heather distract the other Ratchs.

"We have to go, Goldfish," Tellie whispers in my ear.

"But—"

We burst into the hallway and the door slides shut behind us, leaving the others to fight alone.

I know they're tough, and I know they're not afraid, but a sick feeling fills my stomach, like I'm a coward. Like I should be ashamed.

"I have to go back," I say. "I have to."

Georgette takes my face in her hands. They're dry and wrinkly, but her grip is firm. "Listen to me very carefully. We will not win this fight if you stay here. Do you understand me? This is our only chance to stop Ratch. We don't have enough brawn to stop him with our hands, so we have to use our brains. Think about that. Go ahead. You have three seconds."

"One two three," Tellie says in a quick breath. "Now go!"

I let them haul me away, but the sick feeling in my gut stays put.

We nearly run into two robots on our way out, but move quick enough into hiding to dodge them. Twenty-five minutes later, we emerge from the secret tunnel into a half-collapsed warehouse.

The ceiling is open in several spots, letting the sun spill through, illuminating the darkened, hollowed interior. Glass and metal and plastic crunch beneath our feet. Thankfully the building isn't completely gone, so we're able to find a path outside without too much trouble.

I take in a deep breath of fresh air, set my hands on my hips, and turn around.

That's when I see Old New York on the horizon.

Skyscrapers rise up into the sky. I can't tell from here if they're in good shape, or if they're crumbling like the warehouse behind us. Either way, it's still menacing. A place I don't think I want to go.

And it's not just skyscrapers that take up the scene. Crane arms cut through the backdrop of the sky. Some of them are in constant movement, swinging back and

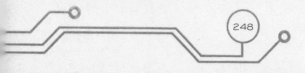

forth, lowering and raising objects I can't make out.

In the center of it all are the points and domes of the Milton Center, where they used to hold weekly competitions that were broadcast over the entire country back before the wars. There were a lot of robot vs. robot bouts, and sometimes man vs. robot, kind of like the fantasy man vs. robot show I watched when I lived in Brack.

The president notices me staring at the building. "That's the facility we need to reach."

I turn to look at him. "*That place?* That's the facility?"

"Do you remember the old vid show that used to be filmed there?" Georgette asks, and I nod. "It was a cover for what went on below ground. And a lot of the robots Cland Industries worked on and developed ended up in the competitions aboveground. It was a good way to test them."

My mouth works, but nothing comes out. I was young when the war started, like seven years old, but I can remember the competitions. Po and I hardly ever liked the same shows, but we loved the Milton shows. I would never have guessed they were making robots below ground in the same building.

"That place is going to be crawling with robots," Tellie says, and her shoulders rock with a shiver. Her dad takes her hand and squeezes.

We start out by foot toward Milton Hall. I'm guessing we're over a half hour away, and my feet already hurt.

"I guess we should talk about what we're going to do once we get to Milton?" I say. "Ratch probably has it on major watch."

"Probably." Georgette pushes hair out of her eyes. "Or maybe he has very few bots on it, because he doesn't want to draw attention to where it's located."

That's what I hope for as we head into the city.

I can kinda remember a time when Old New York was a place everyone talked about as being the best city on earth. Back when it was full of color and people and lights. There were shows on stage. And holo shows in the center of the streets. And Central Park was full of hoverboarders zooming up and down the pathways.

As we cross into the city, into what used to be Manhattan, I'm shocked at how different it is from the memories I have of it on TV.

The hover rails are dead and cracked, at least on the outskirts of the city. Gears and gnarled, twisted wires lay in the street everywhere you look. Sometimes we even happen across an empty robot shell with hollow arm sockets and missing heads.

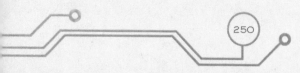

Everywhere I look I can still see the damage from the war. The buildings we pass have holes in the sides from old laser shots. And some buildings aren't even buildings anymore but piles of rubble. It reminds me of how much we have to lose. I don't want Line Zero, or any of the UD, to look like this.

The walk into Manhattan seems to take forever. Every now and then we have to duck inside an old building to avoid bots patrolling the streets, or an army of spider bots like the ones Tellie and I saw in Tallulah.

I feel like there is always someone, or something, watching me here. I don't like it.

When we're finally a block from Milton Hall, Georgette makes us stop for a break. We hunker down in an empty, vine-covered pharmacy. Crushed pills cover the tiled floor. In some spots, they're sticky too, like something was spilled and never wiped up. Mr. Rix sits next to Tellie and wraps his arm around her shoulders, drawing her in. He kisses the top of her head over and over again.

I'm glad we found him. I know Tellie's family isn't close, but I think that's changing. I hate to think of how Tellie would have reacted if she found out Ratch hurt her dad.

"Nathaniel," Georgette says to Mr. Rix, "were you ever inside the facility?"

Mr. Rix shakes his head. "I inherited the code after the war. I've only been inside the facility through a virtual training program. And not a very good one, at that."

"The same can be said for myself," Callo says. "I inherited the code after the last president's term was over."

"All right." Georgette finds a crinkled, water-stained pad of paper and a pencil behind the pharmacy counter. She starts drawing a map. "This is the front entrance to Milton Hall. It faces what used to be Bryant Park. We should assume that way will be heavily guarded. There's a second entrance here, on Thirty-ninth Street. We might be able to get in that way, but if it's guarded too, there is a third entrance reached through the New York Public Library, in the basement. Take the hover rail maintenance line between the two. Sometimes, officials would use that entrance as a way to reach the research facilities without being too conspicuous."

I try to take in everything she's telling me, but it seems like a lot, and there are still a dozen other questions running through my head. My heart is beating so fast, I feel like I might explode at any second. Or go totally nuclear.

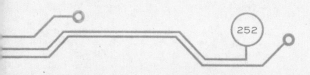

"So . . . are there security checkpoints anywhere between the entrances and the secret facility below ground?" I ask.

Georgette shakes her head. "At least, probably not anymore. There was one checkpoint at the entrance to the lab. But it was sealed long before the wars started, and pretty much forgotten at that. Once Ratch accessed the lab, it essentially broke the seal. It would have to be reprogrammed with new codes."

I look around our group. Tellie, who is skinnier than me, and used to shopping on a daily basis. *Not saving the world.* Mr. Rix, who has spent most of his life in an office. The President of the United Districts, who is . . . *the President of the United Districts.* And Georgette, who is covered in bruises, and has such deep wrinkles around her eyes, they almost take over her face. This is a cracked plan already, and we haven't even started.

I don't know why Po got me free. He should have been the one doing this. Po is the smart one. I'm just good at climbing.

We use the back door of the pharmacy and come out on Thirty-fourth Street. Milton Hall is only a few blocks up.

"We should cross over to Fifth Avenue," Georgette

whispers as we hide behind a broken digital shop sign. There's a bot marching down Thirty-eighth Street ahead. His eyes are trained forward. He seems to have a specific mission, or location, in mind.

Tellie shakes her head. "I think we should go to Sixth Avenue, come back up and go through the library. It's smarter. We'll have more cover."

"But it could be guarded more than any other entrance," Georgette says. "It is, essentially, the most inconspicuous back door of the lab, which would stand to reason, it is the most obvious place to enter. Ratch would know that."

"But LT said it's smarter to take the more obvious route."

My chest knots. Sweat forms on the palms of my hands.

"Trout?" Tellie says. "What do you think?"

"Ummm . . ."

"I think my daughter is right," Mr. Rix says. "And, at this point, any plan is a risky one."

That's true.

A giant bot rounds the corner ahead of us. It's the size of a rhinoceros, with horns on its shoulder armor to match. Its massive head sways side to side, as if it's scanning the streets.

I press my back into the old shop sign, making myself as small as I can. And just when I think we might be safe, it comes down Madison Avenue, which means it'll come right past us.

We're notched.

"Jam," Tellie whispers, her voice hitching like she's about to cry.

The bot gets closer. It's silent save for the whir and click of its interior parts. It must be on some kind of rolling, or hovering, mechanism, because it makes no sound as it moves.

"On the count of three," Georgette says, "run into that store." She points at a storefront where a manikin still stands in the window display, its featureless face pointed at us. "Hide there till the bot passes. Then make a run for Sixth Avenue, like Tellie suggested."

"Wait. Where are you going?" I ask.

Georgette ruffles my hair. It's something Dad and Po do all the time, and mostly I hate it. But not right now. Right now it just makes me sad.

"Do me a favor, Trout? Let Linda rest in peace. I don't want to know what happened to her, but . . . I imagine wherever she is in the great beyond, she's happier. She's an old lady, like me. No one should be immortal. Not even robots."

I nod. "Okay. Sure."

"And one more thing, tell my daughter I'm sorry she was dragged into this. Tell her I'm sorry she suffered."

Georgette swallows, her eyes welling with tears.

Right away I know how Ratch got Georgette's part of the code—he hurt her daughter.

It makes me hate him even more. "I will," I promise.

"Thank you." She turns to Mr. Rix and the president. "When you get down to the lab, look for the black tower in the corner of the control room. That's the server. Do you remember?"

Both of them nod. "Shut down the server, right?" Mr. Rix says.

"Exactly. And then dismantle it entirely."

"You don't have to do this," I say.

She starts counting. "One."

The huge rhino bot gets closer.

"Two."

"I'm not leaving you," I say.

"Three." Georgette stands up straight and tall.

The rhino bot twists around, its metal parts scraping together. It sounds like a huge tanker boat scraping against the bottom of the ocean. It's a sound that makes my teeth wrinkle.

"Come and get me," Georgette screams.

Tellie takes hold of my shirt and drags me toward the store as dozens of spider bots cascade down the front of a brick building heading right for Georgette.

"We can't leave her!" I say to Tellie, but we're already inside the store. And when the door clicks closed behind us, it's like the whole world out in the street disappears. In here, it's cold, and quiet, and smells like layers of dust. There are no rhino bots. No spider bots. No bots at all.

I have a flash of Georgette in my mind, of her being attacked by a hoard of spiders, and it makes me shiver all over.

She's going to die, I realize, only to save us.

Tellie goes to the front window and pushes aside the blinds. "They're headed down Fifth Avenue. We should be clear in about five minutes."

Can we do this? I wonder. I suck in a deep breath. I helped save Edge Flats from Beard and the UD. Just like Po said, I'm capable of a lot more than I give myself credit for.

We *can* do this. I can't let Georgette's sacrifice go to waste.

TWENTY-SEVEN

W E MAKE IT over to Sixth Avenue, then backtrack to Fifth through a department store called Psyler's. It's three floors of boxes and empty clothing racks. The front of the shop is nothing but glass, so we get a good look at what we have to deal with before we dodge across the street to the public library.

As Mr. Rix and the president go to the other end of the store to get another view, Tellie and I scan the roofs of the buildings across the street, checking for signs of spider bots.

In the distance, something flies in the sky, hovering back and forth, like it's scanning the streets. I think it might be a helicopter, but I can't be sure. Probably something else designed by Ratch and his team of rogue robots. I just hope it stays there, on the other side of the city.

Two human-sized robots walk down Fifth Avenue, guns propped on their shoulders.

"Let's wait till they're a block away, then we'll go for it," I say to Tellie.

She nods. "I was thinking the same thing."

We look at each other. "Yeah, but I came up with it," I say.

She rolls her eyes. "You are such a gearbox."

"Yeah well, you're—"

"Totally wrenched," she answers for me.

Mr. Rix comes back without President Callo. "We have a problem."

I look over his shoulder to Callo slumped on the floor, hidden behind a tower of boxes. "What happened?"

"I think he has some internal bleeding," Mr. Rix says. "He isn't doing very well."

"Oh, crack," I say.

"That's not the worst of it. There's another group of bots coming straight for us."

"So now what?" Tellie asks.

Mr. Rix exhales. In the sunlight pouring through the windows, I can better see the dozens of fine lines around his eyes. I never realized until now how tired and old he looked. Or maybe it's just the stress of this whole thing. Maybe the wrinkles are new, maybe they just appeared this morning.

"I'll distract them," he says, and glances at Tellie.

"You two go to the library. When this is all over, send someone for the president."

"No." Tellie grits her teeth. "I came all this way to save you, Daddy."

"I don't see another way," he argues. "I'll find you when it's over. I promise."

But I know that's a promise he can't keep.

"I have another idea." I pull my bag around and unzip it, grabbing the arthropod from inside. "I'll distract them. We don't know how to shut down the tower anyway, Mr. Rix. So you have to go with Tellie."

Tellie almost looks relieved when I point this out.

"Trout," Mr. Rix starts. "I'm not letting a kid do what a man should be doing—"

"I'm almost thirteen." I open the arthropod and slide my arm in. "Besides, this worked once before. It'll work again."

We make sure the president is comfortable and well hidden from sight. As Tellie goes in search of a blanket or sweater to put around him, I crouch next to him. "Is there anything else you need?"

He manages a half smile. "A cheeseburger?"

I laugh. "I'm all out of those."

He closes his eyes and winces when he readjusts. "You are a brave young man, Trout."

Across the store, I watch as Tellie opens a box and pulls out a pink sweater.

"I don't know about that," I respond to Callo.

"No, you are. You and your father and brother. You are great people. The UD needs more people like you."

I think he might be delirious, so I just nod and say thank you.

Tellie comes back with the sweater and tucks it around the president's legs.

"We'll send help as soon as we can," I assure him.

"I'll be fine," he says, and settles into a restless sleep.

At the front door, I peer outside. To Mr. Rix and Tellie, I say, "When I go out, I'll go right, you guys go left. I'll draw them away from you."

Before I open the door, I pull on the pair of Fairenhort goggles I bought before I left Line Zero. They make me feel even more like a soldier.

Not wanting to waste another minute, I whip the door open and step outside. As soon as I'm out on the sidewalk, in the daylight, I regret making the decision to be the distraction. All of the bots in the street, at least thirty of them, turn to me.

"Holy space junk," I breathe.

Too late to turn around.

I start running.

The thunder of robot feet behind me is like the stampede of an army of bulls. I can barely hear the beating of my own heart, even though I can feel it hammering against my ribs.

At the next intersection, I whip my arm out, press the button on the arthropod, and watch as the claw-like hoverpoint shoots out of my hand. It latches itself onto the side of the building across the street, and I'm sucked in like a magnet. I hang there, at least thirty feet off the ground, for a second as I get myself together.

A bot trains his gun on me. I hit the button on the inside of my thumb and plummet to the ground. This is a fall I won't survive.

The ground zooms up beneath me. I hit the button again, and the claw shoots across the street, yanking me back into the air before I hit the ground with a splat.

Before I'm sucked into the hoverpoint, I hit the button again, retract it, hit it again. Soon I'm flying between buildings like Spider-Man, and I can't help but let out a whoop just like he would.

I'm two blocks away from the library when I see something flying in the air toward me. I panic, and miss

hitting the button right away. I fall several feet, arms and legs flailing before I get hold of myself again.

I aim higher with my next shot, and kick my legs, getting some extra momentum so that when I reach the hoverpoint, and hit the button, I fly over the top ledge of an old bakery, and hit the roof and tuck and roll.

I lie there for a second, gravel and old debris digging into my back, when something lands on the roof next to me.

A pair of boots thump toward me and I know in an instant, I'm jammed.

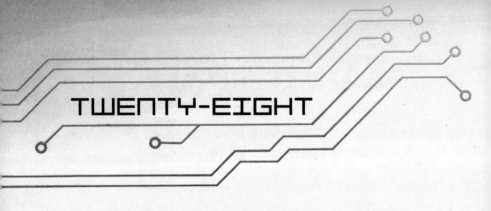

TWENTY-EIGHT

I ROLL OVER ONTO all fours and heave myself up, ready to fight. Except it isn't Ratch on the rooftop with me, or any other bot. It's Vee.

"Holy jet smoke," I say, and collapse against her in relief, our matching arthropods clanging together. "I thought I was dead."

She laughs. "Happy to see you too, FishKid."

I pull away and take off my goggles. "How did you find me? How did you even get here?"

"I traced the disposable Link I gave you. I uploaded it with a tracker app before giving it to you. And I drove, gearbox."

"For once, I'm happy someone did something without telling me!" I raise my arms to the blue sky and thank every hidden star.

"Where is everyone else?" Vee asks as she tucks

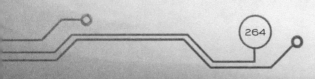

a stray hair into her ponytail. She's not wearing her feather earring, or any necklaces or bracelets. This is fighter Vee.

"Tellie and her dad are in the library trying to stop the ThinkChip control server."

Vee looks past me, out over the city. In the distance, a plume of smoke hits the air and I wonder if that's a point for us or for the bots. I wonder where Po is, if Dad is okay. Are they free on the streets? Are they fighting too?

"We should get to the library to help them," Vee says.

"I don't know how we're going to get inside, though. The streets over there are crowded with bots."

Vee shields her eyes from the sun. "Who said anything about using the streets?"

We make our way back toward Fifth Avenue, but the same bots that were there when I left Tellie are still there, as if waiting for me to return. A short but wide bot charges up his laser gun and takes a shot at us as we sail through the air.

It misses us, but just by a foot.

We aim our arthropods at the library, hit the buttons, and loose the claws through the broken windows. In a second, we're flying through the windows, sucked into

the hoverpoints that are lodged into the walls inside the library.

When I detach my point, I hit the ground hard and grit my teeth, taking an extra second to recuperate. When I finally stand up and look around, I freeze in place, totally in awe. Sunlight blazes through what's left of the arched windows behind us and pools on the patterned floor. An iron lantern still hangs from its chain from the ceiling over the staircase on my right. There are stone columns in front of us. Huge, *huge* columns. The second floor is open through more arches that look down on the first floor.

I wish I were here just to explore.

But I can't.

At least not now.

After a lot of wandering around, we finally locate the stairs down to the basement. Once we're below ground, everything becomes still again. There are rows upon rows of shelves on the first below-ground floor. Most of the shelves are empty, but books remain here and there, some stacked up on top of each other in piles that look as though they could crash at any second.

Vee gestures to a plastic sign glued to the wall. It reads *To Bryant Park Storage,* with an arrow pointing us

in the right direction. So we follow the signs to an open door where cobwebs still hang.

"I hate spiders." Vee runs her hands up and down her arms.

"I hate moths."

She snorts. "Moths? Are you cracked?"

I frown. "Moths are scary! They eat sweaters!"

She bursts out laughing. "That is the best thing I've heard all day."

"Whatever."

We peer into total darkness.

"I'll go first," I say.

Once inside, I'm totally disoriented. Somehow it feels darker *in* the tunnel, like the blackness inside is liquid that swallowed me up. The hair on my neck stands straight.

"Here, take my hand," I whisper to Vee.

Fingers slide into my hand, but they aren't warm, human fingers.

They're cold. And metal. And they bite into my palm. Blood wells in fresh crescent-moon cuts and I swallow the yelp trying to escape me.

"I know where we're going," Ratch says. "How about I lead the way?"

TWENTY-NINE

I'M THROWN BACK, out of the tunnel, and smash into a shelving unit. Pain shoots up my back. The shelf teeters back and forth. If it goes down, it's taking the whole row with it, like dominos.

I slump to the floor. Vee screams as one of Ratch's robots holds her in place.

"Did you really think it would be that easy?" Ratch says.

Something coppery fills the spaces between my teeth. It's blood, I realize and spit it out.

"The problem with humans," he starts, "is that they believe they can conquer anything. They believe they are smarter than the enemy. Stronger too. Maybe that's true in a human war, but I'm a robot, Trout. I will always be smarter and stronger. And I don't have any human emotions holding me back."

My vision sways. Pain throbs behind my eyes. I

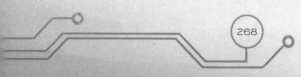

worry I have a concussion. What are the symptoms of a concussion?

Ratch paces in front of me. I have to get it together. Otherwise we're all done for.

"I have to give you credit, though," he says. "You made it this far. Farther than any grown man did. Like your father. Weak. Useless. Neither man, nor robot. When all of this is over, I plan to make your father my slave."

Something inside of me snaps. Rage boils through my veins. I grit my teeth. I make it to my feet.

I feel like I'm about to go nuclear.

I clench my hands into fists and charge.

Ratch isn't prepared for it, and I take him down with my momentum. We slide forward, toward the tunnel entrance. Ratch's back leaves a long gouge in the stone floor.

I roll away. A bot lunges for me, but I'm small and quick and he's got no shot.

I charge at the bot holding Vee hostage. He doesn't move. Probably because he's under Ratch's control and Ratch is currently distracted.

"Run, Trout!" Vee says, but I'm not leaving her, and she's a bolt-head if she thinks I'd do something like that.

I scoop up a huge book. "Duck!" Vee ducks, giving

me a perfect shot at the bot's head. I whack him where it counts and his neck snaps back. His head cranks to the side. I hit again and his claw-like hands let go of Vee's arms.

"Go. Go!" I drag her into the stacks.

"Find them!" Ratch yells.

I go right, then left, then right again, hoping to lose them in the maze of stacks. But then the shelves end, and we have to dodge across a corridor into another room.

The floor here is covered in crumbling newspapers. More line the rows and rows of metal bookcases. I motion Vee down a short aisle and have her sit in the corner. I position myself so I can see the door through the shelving units. So far so good.

I don't know how long we'll stay here. I don't know what my plan is at all. I just need to think. I squeeze my eyes shut for a fraction of a second until I feel Vee tugging at the hem of my shirt.

"What?" I whisper, and she points at the bookcase in front of me, at a shelf above my head.

I look up into the eyes of a spider bot.

"Jam," I breathe one second before it leaps.

The spider bot latches onto my face, its legs wrapped around my head. I can't see at all, so I use my hands,

clawing at the spider with all I got. I tear off one leg and toss it to the side, then work on another, breaking them off one by one like crab legs.

I get the spider off just in time to see the room swarmed with another three dozen of them. They scuttle across the floor together, like one mass being.

Vee gives the bookcase behind her a push. The units here aren't as huge as the ones in the main stacks, so it doesn't take much to tip it over. It creaks, groans, then crashes into the next unit and spider bots are thrown every which way.

The rest of the cases go down too, until the last smashes through the room's back wall and into the main part of the basement.

"Go! Go!" I say, and Vee scrambles over the bookcases. I race after her, the spider bots following.

We burst into the main part of the library, and are greeted by three bots, their laser guns trained right on us. The barrels glow orange in the dim light. I tense, knowing there's only a second, maybe two, before they pull the triggers and blast us out of this world.

"We are so cracked," Vee says.

And then all three bots pitch to the side, matching holes in their heads belching smoke.

I look to the right. Scissor stands in an aisle of shelves,

shoulders squared, a laser gun at her side. Her audience track claps as her LED panel glows bright yellow.

"How did you—" I start, but Vee cuts me off.

"No time!"

Ratch rounds the corner. Scissor throws Vee a laser gun and Vee starts shooting.

Spider bots swarm us. I lunge for a laser gun abandoned by one of the dead bots and press the trigger at the last second. One spider bot disintegrates in front of me. I shoot again, blasting a spider clear down the corridor.

I shoot again and again, taking out spider bots like they're the enemies in a vid game.

Ratch goes for Scissor first. "I see you are still in charge of your own ThinkChip?"

Scissor backs away. "I upgraded my chip this morning, because I'm smarter than you." Her audience track goes *oooooooh*.

Ratch grabs Scissor's arm and bends it back at an odd angle. Scissor's free hand retracts into her arm, leaving nothing but a metal spike in its place. She stabs upward, burying the spike into Ratch's side. He convulses, falls to his knees.

"I suggest you get moving!" Scissor says to us.

Vee pushes the barrel of her gun into the gut of the

spider and says, "Look away, FishKid," right before she blasts the spider with one shot. It bursts into a million plastic and metal pieces. I shield my face with an arm, but several pieces get through, slicing open the skin on my cheeks. Blood instantly runs from the cuts.

"Thanks," I say.

"Don't mention it." She nods toward the tunnel entrance. "You first?"

"I'm on it," I say, and run into the tunnel.

We run down the darkened tunnel, following its many curves. When we reach the secret facility beneath Milton Hall, I find Tellie and her dad in the room, but they aren't alone.

They're both being held by robots, but not just any robots. Robots made of black composite with a band of orange eyes.

I have a gun in my hand, but I know I'm not fast enough to outdo a robot. More importantly, I don't know if I'm a good enough shot to hit Ratch's clones without harming Tellie or Mr. Rix.

I look around the room for another weapon, or a distraction.

The facility is exactly like I thought it would be.

It's about the size of my old house in Brack. A control panel runs the span of the room straight across from the door we entered. Lights blink on the boards. Mostly red. Some blue.

There are a few desks in the center covered in dust. Fluorescent lights hang from the ceiling by thin chains.

The server, pushed into the back corner, is taller and skinnier than me. A row of lights blaze in the top panel. A screen below that reads OUTPUT 100%.

I can't tell if there's an off switch, which I guess would make it too easy.

Something zips into the room behind Vee and me. I think it's Scissor, and turn around, but a hand grabs me by the throat and slams me on the ground. I lose the ability to breathe. Vee shouts something that I can't make out over the ringing in my head.

Orange eyes come into view. It's Ratch's hand wrapped around my throat, closing off my airway. My lungs burn. My throat turns raw.

"Now, Tellie!" Mr. Rix says.

Tellie goes limp, dropping to the floor, taking her robot down with her. Mr. Rix swings back, breaking the knee of his robot. Vee swoops in and blasts Tellie's bot with the laser gun. My nose fills with the smell of charred rubber.

Ratch lifts me up. My feet leave the ground. I'm close

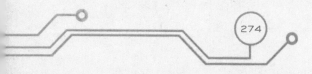

enough to him that I can see the finer details in his head and neck, close enough that I can see the patched charcoal metal exactly where LT said it would be.

It's the *real* Ratch.

He smashes me against the server. My eyes water. I grit my teeth against the pain taking over every corner and nook of my body.

I'm dead. Notched. Ratch is going to kill me. He's going to win.

His metal teeth mash together. "It's really nothing personal, Trout. You're just collateral damage in the laying of the framework. The country has been divided for too long, and it's time to unify it under one robot ruler."

"Under you?" I choke out. "You'll never be a leader."

Some odd emotion crosses Ratch's face. He shakes his head and starts to say something as a sharp object bursts from his sternum. Wires snap and spark inside Ratch's torso. He looks down at the chair leg jammed straight through him, through his hard drive. I can just make out the top of Tellie's head over Ratch's shoulder.

Ratch jolts. His fingers lose function and he lets me go. "This is not how this was supposed to end," he says.

I slump to the ground as he pitches forward, slamming into the server tower. Tellie cocks her arm back.

She holds a folded chair over her head and swings it, hitting the other end of the chair leg still sticking out of Ratch's back. It jams forward, slicing through the innards of the server tower.

Wires catch fire. Smoke curls from the wreckage. Ratch's body seizes and shakes uncontrollably. The ceiling lights flicker, then cut out as sparks from Ratch's body illuminate the darkness.

I pull myself up and gulp down air. Everything hurts. I can barely keep my eyes open. What about the other clones? Are they dead? Are we safe? All I can smell is the scent of burning plastic and rubber. It hurts my nose. Makes me nauseous.

"Trout?"

I think that's Tellie.

Something buzzes in my ears.

"Aidan."

A spindly hand grabs the front of my shirt and yanks me closer. "Aidan," Ratch says, his voice raspy, urgent. Only a flicker of orange light shines in his eyes.

I fight against his hold. The room spins. Someone else calls my name.

"Take my black box," Ratch instructs. "It's in my back, in the lower right quadrant. Give it to LT. You . . ." He shudders again, clamps down his teeth. Then his

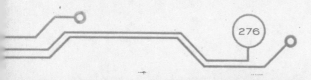

fingers loosen and his head slumps against the tower.

I start to move away but groan at a sudden, sharp pain in my side.

"Don't move," Tellie says. "We're getting help."

"The box," I say.

"What?" she asks.

I close my eyes and hear soft music playing beside me. It's Scissor. "The box," I tell her. "Get Ratch's black box."

"Ratch beat him up real bad," Vee answers.

"Let's get him out of here."

Get the box, I think. Starbursts bloom behind my eyes. I sink lower and lower. Or at least it feels that way.

"FishKid, can you hear me?"

Yes. I want to say yes, but my lips won't work.

The starbursts disappear and everything goes dark.

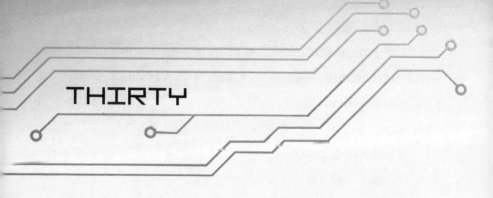

THIRTY

IT'S HARD TO open my eyes, and when I finally do, I have to slam them shut again from the blinding white light. I must be dying, I think, and then I hear harps and violins and gear out for real, because that's what I imagine angels playing at the gates to heaven.

"Scissor," Dad says, "is that necessary?"

"Oh, sorry." The harp music cuts out.

I slowly open my eyes again.

First thing I see is Po leaning over me. A black patch covers his right eye. Bruises pepper his jaw. Behind him is Dad, arms crossed over his chest. His metal faceplate is still dented and caved in around his cheekbones.

On the other side of the bed are Scissor, Marsi, Vee, Tellie, Parker, Mr. Rix, and—

"LT!" I squeak, my voice raw and scratchy. Everyone laughs.

"It is nice to see you too, Trout." He smiles and shifts, and that's when I notice his empty arm socket.

I swallow real hard. "Sorry. About your arm. I didn't mean . . ."

"Scissor will patch me up soon enough."

Scissor nods. "I have many arms to choose from. Blue arms. Red arms. Metal and rubber arms—"

"A metal arm will be all I require."

Scissor waves that idea away, like it's the silliest thing she's ever heard of. "Boring."

Tellie takes my hand in hers. "Are you okay?" Her eyes are bloodshot and her cheeks tearstained.

I try to move but cringe against the pain in my back. "Umm . . . I think so?"

"Stay put," Dad orders. "You have several cracked ribs. You'll be lying there for a while."

Remembering what Ratch did to me wakes me up all the way. "Is Ratch . . . did he . . . the box—"

"He's dead," Po answers. "And Scissor got his black box."

"And the ThinkChips? The clones?"

"It's all under control," Dad says. He comes to my side and pushes the hair away from my forehead. "You need to rest and stop worrying about everything else for a bit. Got it, son? Stop trying to save the world."

I grin real big. "But it's what I do best."

That makes everyone laugh again.

Which makes me cringe real hard from the pain.

"Nurse!" Dad calls.

A guy in his twenties hurries into the room. He's wearing a gray hospital uniform. The pocket on his chest says *New Mercy Medical*.

I'm in a hospital. And there are machines surrounding me. Which means we have power again.

Thank god.

We won.

We really won.

"Can you give him something to knock him out?" Dad asks. "Before he runs off trying to save the whales or something?"

"Umm . . ." The nurse purses his mouth as he thinks about it.

"Dad, come on! I'm not going anywhere."

Dad doesn't listen to me. Vee gives me a look that says she feels bad for me.

"I suppose we could," the nurse answers.

"I don't need anything . . ."

The nurse disappears again.

"Dad," I try. "I can barely talk. Like I'm going to try to escape."

"This is for your own good."

The nurse comes back. Dad moves out of the way as the nurse sticks a needle into the IV tube stuck in my hand.

Vee salutes me. "See you when you wake up, Fish-Kid."

Tellie leans over and plants a kiss on my cheek. "Thanks for everything, Trout."

And then I'm out again.

THIRTY-ONE

DAD MAKES ME stay in the hospital for over a week. Which I guess is fine considering I can barely move anyway. At least in the hospital there's always someone there to wait on me. And I get to watch endless amounts of TV.

Not that all of it is good news.

President Callo was found where Tellie and I left him in the department store in ONY. He was returned to the UD safely, but not without injuries. He suffered a few broken ribs, like I did, a punctured lung and a broken arm. He still made a speech at the UD capitol vowing to find every one of Ratch's clones and dismantle them immediately, regardless of whether or not they were dangerous without their leader.

He also gave his support to Robert St. Kroix and the Meta-Rise, which caused a lot of chaos and cheers and boos from the UD. Dad said he wasn't surprised to

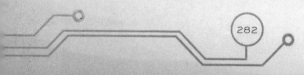

hear such a varying response. "It will take time to have everyone's support," he said.

On my fourth day in the hospital, I get a Link call from Georgette's daughter.

She's older than the girl in the picture I saw in Georgette's house by at least ten years. And she probably looks older still with the bruises peppering her face, and the tired wrinkles framing her eyes.

I curse Ratch all over again for hurting the people he hurt.

"Hello, Trout." She smiles. "You're looking great."

"So are you . . . uh . . ."

I try to remember what her name is. Georgette never talked about her by name, but she's one of Tellie's favorite fashion designers. She talks about her brand all of the time. Something like Harbor Nine, err . . . maybe Nine Harbors. But that still doesn't tell me what *her* name is.

She must see me struggling, because she says, "I'm Nadia, by the way."

"Oh, yeah. Hi!" My voice squeaks, which makes Nadia grin.

"I just wanted to thank you," she says.

I frown and turn down the volume on my TV. "Why? I didn't do anything."

283

"You helped bring an end to a terrible situation."

I remember the look on Georgette's face right before she ran away from me, to distract the rhino bot. She wasn't scared. She was happy. Excited, even. But that expression will always haunt me as the very last expression she made, which makes it sad on its own.

"I don't deserve any thanks," I say, and duck my head. "I should have tried to save your mom."

"You did what you were supposed to do." Nadia shifts, and her bright pink earrings wiggle back and forth.

"She wanted me to tell you something," I say. "She wanted you to know that she was sorry you were dragged into this. That you suffered."

Nadia looks away for a second, and sniffs. Tears glisten in her eyes. "Thank you for that, Trout." She wipes at her eyes with her index fingers and finally looks at me again. "We're having a memorial next week for my mother. I wanted to invite you personally."

"Really?" I sit up straighter. "It would be great to meet you in person. And . . . pay my respects," I add.

She smiles again. "Bring your father and your brother. Bring anyone you'd like."

Before we even hang up, I have it in my head that I'll do something special for Georgette's memorial. I don't

know what, but with Scissor's help, I'm sure we can come up with something great.

We say good-bye, after we chat a little bit more. Which is good, because I can barely keep my eyes open.

When the Link connection winks off, I close my eyes for a second, *just to rest,* I tell myself, but then I'm out.

On my last day in the hospital, I get a special guest.

"Well, there he is," Lox says. "The big hero, once again, saving the world, and you didn't even take me with you! You promised to include me on the next adventure."

I smile and pull myself up in the bed. It's getting easier and easier to move.

"Sorry," I say. "But it's not like I had this mission all planned out and could have warned you ahead of time."

Lox plops into the chair beside my bed. "Sure. Sure. And next you'll tell me going on an adventure with two cute girls was the worst thing you've ever done in your whole entire cracked life."

I snort. "You are unbelievable."

"And you are selfish."

"Next adventure," I promise.

"That's what you said last time, bolt sniffer."

"Well, I double promise this time. Cross my heart."

Lox scratches at the back of his head. "Cross your heart. Like I'm gonna take that seriously."

"You should. I take heart crossing *very* seriously."

And then we both burst out laughing.

When I get out of the hospital, Dad informs me we're heading to Texas, instead of Line Zero. "It's too wrecked," he says. "There's a reconstruction crew working on the major damage now. We'll return when the power grid is back up."

I picture Line Zero like the ghost towns Tellie and I saw on our way to Georgette's, but when I ask Dad about it, he says at least half the citizens stuck around to help with the cleanup, including Parker, Jules, and Cole. When I point out that we should be helping too, he says I'm not good to anyone if I don't get rest.

"And what about the Meta-Rise?" I ask.

He sighs. "The Rise has a lot of work ahead of it. A few days isn't going to make or break the cause."

We head to Edge Flats, to Dekker's house, all of us—Dad, Po, Marsi, Vee, and me—squeezed into one car. The drive takes forever. Mostly because we have to keep stopping for the girls. Vee can only go like an hour

before having to use the bathroom, which probably has something to do with all the purple slushies she's been drinking. And Marsi likes to get out and stretch every now and then, since the muscles that were damaged where she was shot seize up sometimes.

When we reach Dek's house, he greets us at the front door, his rainbow hair half tied back with a rubber band.

"I've missed you, little dude!" he says, and gives me a light hug, careful around my ribs.

"Missed you too, Dek."

He hugs Vee next, squeezing her real tight. "Little missy dude. Glad to have you hanging out for a bit."

Vee smiles up at him. "I'm glad to be here."

He looks past us at Po and Marsi. "What happened to you?" he asks Po.

Po is still wearing his eye patch. When I left him in the tunnel of the old research facility, he got banged up real bad at the hands of Ratch. Something happened to his eye. He won't talk about it, not yet, but Scissor has been working on him every few days. That can only mean one thing—that whatever happened to him, it was bad enough that the only way to fix it was to use technology and machines.

Po manages to dodge Dek's questions, instead asking about LT in the far corner of the living room, where he's manning a wall of computers. "He crack Ratch's black box yet?"

Dek leans in and whispers, "Not yet, but he's a man on a mission. Or should I say, *metalman* on a mission."

"I heard that," LT says.

"You need any help?" Dad asks.

"No, thank you." LT swivels around just enough to wave at us. "Go enjoy the family. I will take care of this."

He doesn't have to tell us twice.

Tellie comes into town later that night, bags packed. She spent the last week with her mom and dad, doing nothing but being a family, she said. It makes me happy, hearing that. I'm glad the Rix family is getting along better. She's coming to stay with us while her parents dive back into work. Her mom is covering the botched robot takeover, and even scored an exclusive interview with the president.

Now we sit at the kitchen table, two Bot-N-Bolts shakes in front of us.

"Did you see your mom before you left?" I ask, running my finger through the condensation on my glass.

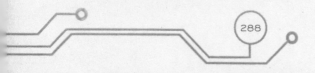

"No. She had to fly out to Second District early this morning, but we talked through vid this afternoon."

I take a sip of my shake. The straw hits an empty spot and gurgles. "What about school? Are you going to go here?"

She shrugs. "I don't know. What are you doing?"

"My dad hasn't said yet. School in Line Zero is out for a while. Until things are cleaned up."

"Maybe we should both go to the public school here in Texas. Could be fun."

I snort. "Yeah, fun like when we went to school together in Brack?"

She snickers. "I'm not that girl anymore, Goldfish! Can't you give me a second chance?"

"I don't know," I say sarcastically. "We'll see." I down the rest of my shake and take the glass to the sink. I rinse it out and stick it in the dishwasher because I know Dek hates dirty dishes in the sink. I turn around, only to find Tellie standing right behind me.

"I'm glad we're friends now, Trout. And I'm sorry I ever ignored you in Brack. I wasn't very nice back then."

I shrug. "We've all changed."

"That's true. Now you're totally wrenched."

"I don't know about that."

"It's true. If you went back to Brack, you'd be the most popular kid there."

I look away, feeling heat rising in my cheeks.

Before I know what's happening, she's leaning toward me, planting a kiss on my lips. "Thanks for everything, Goldfish." She walks away and disappears upstairs to the third floor.

I stand there in the middle of the kitchen for a second, not blinking, or breathing, until I hear snickering from the staircase leading down to the living room. It's Dek and Po.

"I can hear you guys," I say.

They burst into the room, laughing their fool heads off.

"He just froze!" Po says. "Like an icicle. His first kiss and he froze!"

"Sorry, little dude," Dek says. "But you looked so lost."

"It wasn't my first kiss!" I argue. Well, technically it was, but I'm not going to admit that.

I drop into one of the chairs at the table and sulk. Po comes over a second later and pats me on the top of the head.

"Paybacks, little brother. Paybacks."

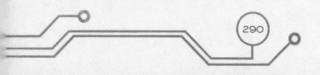

"Whatever," I say, but inside I feel all weird and squirrely and . . . well, happy. I turn away from my brother and Dek, because of the silly smile I feel spreading across my face.

Tellie Rix just kissed me.

If this is what saving the world gets me, I could get used to it.

ACKNOWLEDGMENTS

Always, I must thank my husband, JV, for being there, for supporting me, for talking me off the ledge, for letting me sleep in, for bringing home loads of caffeine, and knowing exactly how to make me laugh.

Many thanks (and many many more) to Joanna Volpe, for being the awesomest agent ever.

My editor, Kate Harrison, for knowing how and when to push me, to make Trout's story even better.

To everyone else at Dial Books and New Leaf Literary, for being the force behind and beyond the book.

Huge thanks to my parents and mother-in-law, for endless hours of babysitting. Without them, this book would be nothing but a puddle of tears and empty chocolate wrappers.

Erica O'Rourke, and her daughter, for their kind words and support!

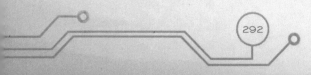

Patricia Riley, Danielle Ellison, and Kari Olson for being the greatest long-distance friends a girl could ask for.

Lucy—the greatest BESTIE EVER.

Jen Merchant, for being LT's biggest fan!

To the entire online community—without them, I would just be a girl, alone in her office, in her yoga pants, talking to herself (and eating junk food).

And lastly, to all the readers, past, present, and future. Thank you for joining Trout on his adventures.